Sam snuck into the empty ⟨...⟩ made straight for McCrack⟨...⟩ What if it's locked? she wondered.

But the drawer slid open easily. She took out the file marked MATH TESTS and began to skim through it. It was a thick file with dozens of tests. And at the very end of it was another file labeled ANSWER SHEETS.

Sam felt her pulse race. This was excellent! It was exactly what she was looking for!

"Hurry!" Sylvie called frantically from outside the door. "Someone's coming!"

Meet all the kids in McCracken's Class:

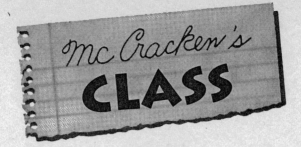

McCracken's CLASS

#7

SAM THE SPY

by Diana Oliver

BULLSEYE BOOKS
Random House New York

To Liz Marraffino,
writer, artist, friend

A BULLSEYE BOOK PUBLISHED BY RANDOM HOUSE, INC.

Copyright © 1994 by Random House, Inc.
Cover design by Michaelis/Carpelis Design Associates, Inc.
Cover art copyright © 1994 by Melodye Rosales. All rights reserved
under International and Pan-American Copyright Conventions.
Published in the United States by Random House, Inc., New York,
and simultaneously in Canada
by Random House of Canada Limited, Toronto.
Library of Congress Catalog Card Number: 93-85236
ISBN: 0-679-85698-6
RL: 4.2

Manufactured in the United States of America
10 9 8 7 6 5 4 3 2 1

MCCRACKEN'S CLASS is a trademark of Random House, Inc.

Samantha Tillman slumped against the hall-way end table as she watched her mother go through her morning routine. Dressed for work, Ms. Tillman set her briefcase, purse, and newspaper on the hall table. Then she put on her winter coat and a long scarf.

"I've got a school budget meeting tonight, sweetheart," Ms. Tillman said. "So I'll probably be a little late."

Sam nodded sadly. Her mother was the principal of a nearby public school, Martin Luther King, Jr., Elementary. She was almost always "a little late"—which meant she rarely came home before eight at night.

Ms. Tillman reached into her purse, took out ten dollars and a pink receipt, and handed them to Sam. "Would you pick up my dry cleaning for me? And straighten up the living room, please. I want all those videos back in the cabinet where they belong."

Sam brushed back a shock of brown hair from her face. "Why don't you hire a maid? Danielle has one," she said, before she could stop herself. Immediately, she regretted what she'd said—and how she'd said it. She didn't really mind doing chores. She just didn't like doing them all by herself.

Ms. Tillman sighed as she buttoned her coat. "Danielle also has a limousine and a chauffeur. Your friend comes from a wealthy family. You know your father and I don't have that kind of money. We're already paying a lot for your school. The last thing we need is another expense right now. Besides, the three of us are perfectly capable of cleaning up after ourselves."

"I know, Mom. Sorry," Sam mumbled. Lately, her parents were always complaining about how much her school cost. Sam went to Parkside Academy for Girls, a ritzy private school just a few blocks from the brownstone where the Tillmans lived. Her parents said a year at most colleges was cheaper than a year at the Academy.

"There's a casserole in the freezer you can microwave for dinner," her mother continued. "And make sure you do your homework before watching TV."

Sam nodded, not really listening. She'd

heard it all before. She could recite it from memory.

Her mother leaned down and kissed her. "I'm sorry things are so rushed, darling. Things will be more relaxed when your father gets back."

Sam said nothing. She knew things were no calmer when her dad was around. Her father owned a small computer software company. He was every bit as busy as her mother. Now he was in Europe, meeting with European computer companies. Last night he had flown to Brussels. Sam couldn't help but picture her dad knee-deep in brussels sprouts. Thinking about it made her feel a bit better.

Her mother started out the front door, then turned back. "Sam," she said, "I'm sorry I've been so busy lately—"

"It's okay," Sam said, reaching up to kiss her. It really wasn't okay, but Sam didn't want to start a fight before her mother left. If she did, she'd feel bad for the rest of the day.

Sam watched her mother walk down the stairs of the brownstone to the street. *How can I be related to someone who looks like that?* she wondered for the umpteenth time. Her mother was tall and slender. She always wore neat, elegant clothing that looked exactly right. Her smooth, glossy hair framed her face perfectly. Her earrings and bracelets always matched. Nothing about Alexandra Tillman was ever out of place.

Sam went over to the mirror and straightened her school uniform. Even though she'd just put it on an hour ago, it was already a mess. She'd buttoned the red knit vest wrong. There was a spot on the navy blazer. And the white blouse was pulling out of the waistband of the plaid skirt.

Sam studied her reflection. She had her mother's dark hair and dark eyes, but the two of them didn't look alike. Her mother was built like a fashion model. Sam was built like a munchkin. She had always been the shortest kid in her class. Although Sam was in the fifth grade, she looked like she should have been in the third. Kids were always teasing her about it. Her pediatrician said she was normal. He promised she would grow. But Sam had her doubts.

Sam straightened her uniform and put on her down jacket. Then she grabbed her books, locked the door, and set off for Parkside Academy. Even though it was wintertime and a Monday, she loved the walk to school. The Tillmans lived on Chestnut Street, in one of Parkside's nicest neighborhoods. The streets were lined with elegant three-story brownstones. Most of them were built in the 1800s. Almost every house had a garden and a gas lamp in front. In the evenings, Sam liked to pretend that when she turned onto her street, she was stepping back in time into an older, quieter city.

But what Sam liked best about her neighborhood was the Parkside Academy for Girls. The private school was housed in what had once been a Georgian mansion. It was a huge, white building with tall, white columns on the outside and a fireplace in nearly every room.

As Sam approached the school, a guard opened the wrought-iron gate for her. Sam cut across the wide lawn to the main building. Her feet made a crunching sound on the frost-covered lawn.

She stepped across the marble-floored entry. Even though Sam had attended the Academy since kindergarten, she still loved the feeling of entering the beautiful old building. For a school, it was a pretty cool place.

Since she had ten minutes before class began, she hurried to the student lounge. The lounge had once been one of the mansion's drawing rooms. Now girls gathered in small groups, sitting on the windowsills or in the old carved chairs in front of the fire.

Sam headed straight for her best friend, Danielle Vaughn. Danielle and another girl in their class, Mia Sand, were sitting in a corner of the room. Mia's family was from Quebec, and Mia made everyone pronounce her last name "Saaand." Sam had been taking French since the third grade, so she understood that that was the proper way to pronounce it. Still, she thought Mia was a little stuck-up.

Danielle and Mia sat with their heads bent over an open newspaper. Danielle glanced up as Sam approached. "Congratulations," she said. "You're famous."

"I am?" Sam said, surprised. Lots of her classmates actually were famous. Or at least their parents were. Danielle's mother was a major fashion model. Mia's dad played pro hockey.

Danielle handed the paper to Sam. Sam saw that it was the *Parkside Weekly,* the free local paper. It was opened to the editorial page.

"Henry had this in the car," Danielle explained. Henry drove the limousine that took Danielle to school every morning. "He said there was a letter to the editor about you and your mom."

Sam skimmed the letter quickly. It was

about Martin Luther King, Jr., Elementary. The writer talked about how in the three years since Sam's mother had become principal, MLK, Jr., had become one of the best public schools in the city. The letter ended, "If MLK, Jr., is such a good school, then why won't its principal let her own daughter attend? Samantha Tillman, the principal's eleven-year-old daughter, attends Parkside Academy for Girls. Does Ms. Tillman think her daughter is too good for our school?"

"Of course, she is!" Mia said with a laugh.

Danielle looked pained. "Can you imagine?" she asked. "Going to MLK, Jr.?"

Sam thought about it for a minute, picturing the squat, ugly brick building, covered with graffiti.

On the one hand, she felt proud of the school. Her mother really had worked hard to make MLK, Jr., a better place. But better wasn't good enough for Danielle, Mia, or Sam.

"No way," she answered as the bell for the first class rang. "I'd rather die."

That evening Sam sat at the kitchen table, listening to the hall clock, chime. It was nine P.M. She'd straightened up the living room. She'd eaten her microwave casserole. Her homework was almost done. Though she'd never admit it, the house felt lonely with both her parents out.

Sam heard someone coming up the front stairs. She peeked through the window panel next to the door. Then she threw open the door and hugged her mother as she entered the hallway.

"Hello, sweetheart," her mother said, running a hand through Sam's hair.

"You're really late," Sam said.

"For a change," her mother agreed wearily. She laid her briefcase on the end table and took off her coat. "Did you have your dinner?"

"Everything's taken care of," Sam

reported. "Will you sit with me in the kitchen?"

"Of course I will," her mother replied, placing an arm around Sam's shoulders.

But as Sam finished her homework, she could tell that her mother wasn't really paying attention. She was glancing through a file she'd taken from her briefcase.

"Done!" Sam said, as she finished translating her last sentence.

Her mother kept reading.

"Mom," Sam said.

"Just a minute, sweetie. Let me finish this report."

Sam sighed loudly and waited for her mother to stop reading. At last her mother looked up.

"Did you see the letter in the *Weekly?*" Sam asked.

"Yes," Ms. Tillman answered. "Sooner or later someone was bound to complain about our sending you to the Academy. I'm sorry you're getting dragged into something that's really about my job."

Sam shrugged. "It's no big deal," she said. "It actually made me kind of famous at school. Everyone wanted to talk to me about it."

Ms. Tillman smiled. "My daughter, the

eleven-year-old celebrity."

"Mom," Sam began hesitantly, "speaking of the kids at school, there's something I've been wanting to ask."

"What's that?" her mother said, her eyes straying back to the file.

"Could I have my own cellular phone?"

Her mother stopped reading and stared at Sam.

"Excuse me?" she said.

Sam hated it when her mother pretended not to have heard her correctly.

"I think I need my own cellular phone," Sam explained, "so I can talk to my friends whenever I want to. The phones in the living room and kitchen are used by the whole family. And the one in the study is just for you, and the one in your bedroom is just for you and Dad and—"

"No," her mother said.

"Just listen," Sam said. "If I had a portable phone in my room, with my own number, then you could just phone me if you were in your study and wanted me to do something."

"I have no problem shouting up the stairs," her mother pointed out.

"Don't you think that's sort of...tacky?" Sam asked. "Danielle's had her own phone for two months, and Mia got one last week, and—"

Ms. Tillman rubbed the bridge of her nose. "So that's what this is all about," she said, sounding even more tired. "Samantha, how many times do I have to explain that we don't have the kind of money that some of your classmates have?"

"I know that, Mom," Sam said. "But portable phones don't cost all that much and—"

The Tillmans' phone rang at that moment, and Sam's mother went to get it. "Jack!" she said.

For a while, Sam forgot about their argument. Her father was on the phone, calling from Brussels. She listened to her mother's half of the conversation, waiting eagerly for her own turn to talk.

On Friday afternoon at five thirty, Danielle Vaughn's limousine pulled up in front of the Tillman's brownstone. Danielle and Sam had just spent the last two hours at the local skating rink. Henry, the chauffeur, had sat on the side of the rink, watching them and looking very bored.

"See you Monday," Danielle said as Sam climbed out of the limo. "Call me this weekend, okay? Don't forget now."

"I'll call you tomorrow," Sam promised. "'Bye, Danielle. 'Bye, Henry."

"See you, brat," Henry said. Henry called Danielle and all of her friends "brat." He was an older man with salt-and-pepper hair. He was kind of cranky, but Ms. Vaughn wouldn't let Danielle go anywhere without him.

Sam watched as the limo headed back toward the house in the Heights where Danielle and her mother lived. Then she turned toward her own house. The lights were on, she noted happily. For once her mother was home first.

Sam let herself into the brownstone. "I'm home," she called out as she took off her coat.

"I'm on the phone, honey," her mother called from the study. "Be with you in a minute."

Sam took her books upstairs to her room, but she didn't start on her homework. After all, she had the whole weekend to do it. Instead, she went back downstairs to see what was on TV. She spent a few minutes channel-surfing with the remote control. There was nothing on that she wanted to watch. Who was her mother talking to anyway? she wondered. She'd said she'd only be a minute! It was more like fifteen.

Curious, Sam tiptoed through the first floor of the house toward her mother's study. The floors in the Tillmans' house were made of old wooden planks that creaked and squeaked and groaned. But Sam moved soundlessly. When she was four, Sam had had a nightmare that someone evil had broken into their house. In the dream she'd had to sneak out of the house to get help. But the robber heard her footsteps and killed everyone in her family. The dream left Sam terrified. Every day she'd practiced until she could walk through the house without making a sound.

Silently, she crept up to the door outside her mother's study. Sam could see her mom through the glass-paneled door. Ms. Tillman sat at her desk, talking into the phone, occasionally glancing at the screen on her computer.

Sam wished she could pick up one of the other phones, but she knew her mother would be able to hear her do it. So she wedged herself behind the big Chinese vase filled with dried flowers that sat outside the study door. It was her favorite hiding spot—the perfect place to eavesdrop.

"Oh, Jack," her mother said, "that letter in the *Weekly* has caused serious trouble."

Sam sat up a little straighter. Her mother was talking to her father. Why hadn't she told Sam?

Sam listened more carefully.

"Yes," Ms. Tillman said. Her voice was clearly upset. "The school board called an emergency meeting last night. And it was all about that letter."

Her mother was quiet for a moment as her father responded. Then she said, "Of course, I told them Sam's been at the Academy since kindergarten. And, yes, I told them she started there three years before I started at MLK, Jr. But they're afraid this may turn into a scandal. And they may be right."

Again there was a silence as her father responded. Sam felt herself grow tense.

"Frankly, that meeting got me thinking," Ms. Tillman continued. "After all, MLK, Jr., is a very good school now. The Academy gets more expensive every year. And I don't like what's happening to Sam. Do you know that on Monday she asked why we don't have a maid? Then she wanted to know why I wouldn't buy her her own cellular phone! It might be good for her to be with kids who don't have so much money."

Sam couldn't believe she was hearing this.

"Well," her mother was saying. "Ms.

Rivers's class is full. I'd have to put Sam in Ms. McCracken's class."

Sam's heart began to pound. Not only did her mother want to transfer her to public school, but she wanted to deliver her into the clutches of Ms. McCracken! Sam had heard kids in the neighborhood talking about Crack-the-Whip McCracken. She was the meanest, strictest teacher in all of New York State. Even the tough kids who weren't afraid of anyone were afraid of McCracken.

Sam was clutching the vase so hard she was surprised it didn't shatter in her hands. "Ms. McCracken may be old-fashioned, but she's a good teacher," Ms. Tillman was saying. "She doesn't let her students get away with anything. She might be exactly what Samantha needs."

That did it! Sam bolted out from behind the vase and burst into her mother's office.

"No!" she shouted. "You can't do this!"

On Wednesday morning, Sam sat in the principal's office of Martin Luther King, Jr., Elementary. Her arms were crossed over her chest. Her eyes were fixed on the yellowed, chipped linoleum that covered the office floor. Sam knew she was sulking, but she couldn't help it.

On the other side of the big oak desk, her mother was filling out Sam's enrollment forms.

"That should do it," her mother said cheerfully a few minutes later. She stepped out from behind the desk and held out a hand to her daughter. "Congratulations! It's official. You are now a student at Martin Luther King, Jr.!"

"Thrills," Sam mumbled, still staring at the floor. She felt as if she were starting a prison sentence. The fact that she was wearing a brand-new sweater and leggings instead of a uniform didn't help.

Sam hadn't been away from the Academy for a full day, and already she missed it. She especially missed her friends. She wondered if they missed her.

"Are you feeling all right?" her mother asked in a concerned voice.

Sam wanted to pretend the whole thing was no big deal. Instead, she told her mother the truth. "I'm scared," she said.

"Of what?" Ms. Tillman asked.

Sam couldn't believe her mother didn't know. "I'm scared that all the kids here will hate me as soon as they find out who my mother is."

"I expect some of them will give you a hard time at first," her mother said. "But that won't last long. People will come to know you for who you are."

Sam didn't say anything. Her mother simply didn't understand.

"*I'm* glad you're here," her mother said. "I'm looking forward to seeing a little more of you. Samantha, look at me."

Reluctantly, Sam met her mother's dark eyes. She couldn't stand much more of this.

"I know you're not happy about this transfer," Ms. Tillman said. "But there are many reasons why this change seemed a good idea to your father and me."

"Yeah, you both think I'm not worth it!" Sam shot back. The minute she said it, she was sorry. She was sorry because her mother had been happy a minute ago and now she looked hurt. And she was sorry because it wasn't true. She knew how hard both her parents worked. And she knew that they had always been generous where she was concerned. "Sorry," Sam mumbled.

Ms. Tillman sighed. "I know this is rough for you, honey," she said. "Just try to give this school a chance. There are some wonderful kids in your class. I'm sure you'll make good friends."

"Not like Danielle," Sam argued.

"No, not like Danielle," her mother agreed. "You'll be meeting very different kids here. All right, enough stalling. If I let you sit here any longer, you'll be late for class. And being late is not a good way to start with Ms. McCracken."

Sam groaned as she got to her feet. "I can't believe you put me in McCracken's class," she said for about the fiftieth time. "You should hear what the kids in the park say about her! And it's true, too!"

"I'll hear all about it from you tonight,"

her mother answered. She nudged Sam out the office door. "Come on, I'll take you up to your classroom."

Sam stood rooted to the floor and fixed her mother with a gaze of pure terror. "You can't!" she said.

"Why not?" her mother asked.

"Mom," Sam said. She couldn't believe her mother was so dense. She'd just have to explain. "It's just that...I don't want anyone seeing me with my *mother*."

"Oh," her mother said, obviously trying not to smile. "Of course. I'll have a monitor take you upstairs."

"I can find it myself," Sam said.

"In this school," her mother said in her principal's voice, "new students are escorted to their classrooms. Now would you like to go with me or a monitor?"

"A monitor," Sam said, giving in. She had one last hope for saving herself. "Mom," she said cautiously, "what would you think about me using a different last name?"

"I don't think it's a good idea," her mother answered. "Sooner or later the kids here will find out you're the principal's daughter."

And then they'll hate me, Sam finished silently. *It's going to be hate at first sight.*

A few minutes later, a skinny sixth-grade

boy named Tony Margulies took Sam's file. "This way," he said, heading down the hallway.

The dingy halls were filled with kids on their way to classes. MLK, Jr., definitely had a lot more students than the Academy, Sam noted. The public school was crowded and shabby and ugly. The halls were much louder than what she was used to—but that was probably because of the boys.

It felt weird to be in school with boys suddenly. Not that boys were a big deal or anything. Sam just wasn't used to seeing them in the halls, slamming locker doors, calling out loudly to each other, acting like they owned the place.

"So," she said to Tony, "did you have McCracken last year?"

"Yup," he said, as they started to climb the stairs to the second floor.

"Is she as bad as everyone says?" Sam asked.

"Worse," Tony assured her.

"Worse? How can she be worse? She already sounds like the Wicked Witch of the West."

Tony stopped a short distance from room 206. "Believe me," he said solemnly, "she's the worst. Watch your step."

Sam gulped as Tony opened the door to room 206 and a tall woman with bright orange hair raised her bifocals to glare at them.

"Ms. Tillman, I take it?" the teacher asked.

Sam nodded. Tony handed the teacher Sam's file and took off.

Sam was left staring at the oddest-looking teacher she'd ever seen. At the Academy, most of her teachers were young and dressed stylishly. Ms. McCracken looked like something from a fifties TV show. Her orange hair was teased and sprayed. Sam remembered that one of the kids in the park had called her "Helmet Hair."

She wore an awful avocado-colored dress that clashed with her orange hair and her bright magenta lipstick. Sam wished McCracken were on TV so she could adjust the color.

"Come in, Ms. Tillman," Ms. McCracken said sharply. "I certainly don't intend to conduct class with you standing in the hallway."

"Oh," Sam said, as she practically leaped into the classroom.

There had to be about thirty fifth-graders in the room—and they were all staring at Sam.

"Boys and girls, I'd like you to welcome a new student to our class," Ms. McCracken began. "This is Ms. Tillman."

"Sam," Sam corrected the teacher.

"In this classroom," Ms. McCracken told her, "you will be known as Ms. Tillman."

A few kids laughed.

"Like the principal?" asked a girl with a scar on her mouth.

"Ms. Smith, you should have raised your hand," the teacher said. "But yes, you are correct. The Ms. Tillman who has just joined our class is Ms. Tillman's—the principal's—daughter."

Sam felt herself turn bright red with embarrassment. Why didn't Ms. McCracken just hang a sign on her chest?

"Ms. Tillman," the teacher went on, "would you like to say something to the class?"

Sam gulped. "Not really." Then she looked around the classroom and realized she did have a question. "Uh, actually, I just wanted to know—where are the computers?"

A few kids laughed again, and a few others looked at her as if she'd lost her mind.

Ms. McCracken cleared her throat. "Surely your mother has told you that our school just bought five computers. They will arrive in January of next year."

Sam looked at Ms. McCracken blankly. She usually tuned out when her mother talked about MLK, Jr. Up until now, she wouldn't have cared if her mother said they were buying crocodiles.

"Who gets the five computers?" Sam asked.

"Why the whole school, of course," the teacher answered. "One of the larger storage closets is being converted to a computer room."

"You mean there will be five computers for the *whole school?*" Sam asked. She couldn't believe it. "In the Academy every student has her own desktop terminal. I mean, we all had to share the printers, but we *never* shared computers!"

Ms. McCracken's magenta lips formed a thin line of disapproval. "Then perhaps," she said, "it's time you learned to share. You may take the fifth seat in the fourth row, in front of Mr. Jackson."

Sam saw an empty seat in front of a good-looking boy with skin the color of ebony wood. The boy winked at her, and it was almost as if that wink was his way of telling her it wouldn't be so bad at MLK, Jr., after all.

Sam sat down, relieved that she was no

longer on display in front of the classroom.

"Mr. Jackson, please get Ms. Tillman a science book, a math book, and a history text," Ms. McCracken said.

The boy who sat behind Sam stood up and went over to a green cabinet. Sam felt her mouth drop open with amazement. Mr. Jackson was short! She'd finally met someone in her own grade who was shorter than she was! Maybe McCracken's class wouldn't be so bad, after all.

By the time the morning was out, Sam was depressed again. Not only was she in a computerless school, but MLK, Jr., didn't even teach her favorite subject. She'd sat patiently through science, math, and geography. Then she'd very politely asked Ms. McCracken when the French lesson would begin. Ms. McCracken replied, "You may begin studying a language in the seventh grade."

"Seventh grade?" Sam burst out. This was incredible. "I've been studying French since third grade!"

"I'm *so* impressed," said a boy with blond hair and very blue eyes.

"Mr. Leontes, I'll see you after school," Ms. McCracken said at once. "Ms. Tillman, you'll have to adjust to the fact that our language program begins in the middle school."

My mother has enrolled me in a dive! Sam thought.

A short time later, Ms. McCracken called Sam up to her desk. "I can see from your records that your math and history classes have been slightly more advanced than ours."

"I guess," Sam said.

"A student lacking the proper challenge is a bored student," Ms. McCracken continued. "So I'm going to give you extra homework in those subjects."

"That's not fair!" Sam burst out.

Ms. McCracken peered down her glasses at Sam. "Ms. Tillman, when I want your opinion, I shall ask for it. In the meantime, I will not tolerate students talking back to me. Do you understand?"

Sam nodded, totally miserable.

"Good," Ms. McCracken said. "Here are your extra assignments."

Sam trudged back to her desk and flipped through her homework. For math, she had an extra set of problems—ten of them! For history, she had to write an essay that no one else had been assigned. It wasn't fair! Her new school was definitely a prison!

Sam stood by her locker. She had been dreading her first lunch period at MLK, Jr., almost as much as she'd dreaded McCracken's class. Who was she going to eat with?

"Hi," said a quiet voice at her side. Sam turned to see a blond-haired girl whom McCracken called Ms. Stoppelmeyer.

"I'm Kathleen," the girl said. "I moved here from Pennsylvania a while ago. And I know how it feels to start at a new school. So I thought maybe you'd like to have lunch with me and some of my friends."

Sam smiled for the first time that day. "Sure," she said. "That'd be great."

Sam followed Kathleen to the cafeteria. It didn't smell of cookies and hot chocolate like the dining hall at the Academy. The cafeteria at MLK, Jr., smelled like old ketchup jars. But Sam was so relieved to have someone to sit with that she barely noticed the food.

She got macaroni and cheese, after Kathleen told her it was the safest choice. Then she followed the other girl to a table at the far end of the room. There were already about five other girls seated there whom she recognized from her class.

Kathleen introduced them. "This is Annie Tuzmarti," she said, pointing to a girl with large brown eyes and dark brown hair. Next Kathleen nodded to a girl with coffee-colored skin who wore her long hair in a single braid. "And Desdemona DuMonde."

"Hi," Desdemona said. "I transferred here this year, too."

"From where?" Sam asked.

"From a school in Manhattan," Desdemona explained. "I miss it sometimes."

"And this is Sylvie Levine," Kathleen said, pointing to a red-haired girl who sat beside Desdemona.

"I've gone to school here forever," Sylvie said with a smile.

"And this is Rosa Santiago," Kathleen said.

Rosa was the nerdy-looking girl Sam had noticed sitting at the front of the class. Rosa always raised her hand when the teacher asked a question. As far as Sam could tell,

Rosa always had the right answer.

"This is Sharon Fuller," Kathleen went on, nodding at the girl beside Rosa. "And this is Sasha Sommers," she finished. Sasha was one of the prettiest girls Sam had ever seen, with long, glossy dark hair and small, perfect features.

All in all, none of these girls were as glamorous or sophisticated as Danielle and Mia and the others at the Academy. But they seemed pretty nice.

"So your mother's really the principal?" Sharon asked.

"I guess so," Sam said, unhappily. This was not what she wanted to talk about.

"What's it like?" Sharon asked. "I mean, living with the principal?"

"I don't really know," Sam answered truthfully. "At my other school, we had a different principal. It's only today that I really started thinking of her that way."

"I like your mother," Annie said, taking Sam by surprise. "When I got in trouble, she was really fair."

"She was fair with me, too," Desdemona said. "She's never mean, like my last principal. And she always acts so cool."

Sam grinned. "Well, she's not always cool. She's lost it with me a few times. But for a mother, she's usually okay. She—" Sam stopped speaking as she saw her mother enter the cafeteria. Sam held her breath as her mother gazed around the bustling room. Then, catching sight of Sam, her mother waved and walked toward her.

"There you are, sweetheart," she said as she approached Sam's table. "How is your first day going?"

Once again, Sam thought she'd die of embarrassment. Hadn't she explained things clearly enough to her mother that morning? She needed her space. Why didn't her mother get it?

"Did you enjoy your classes?" her mother asked.

"They were okay," Sam said, frowning.

Her mother gave her a concerned look. "Just okay? What's wrong?"

"Nothing," Sam said, wishing she could crawl under the table and vanish.

"We'll talk about it tonight," her mother promised before she swept off.

"You know," Annie said thoughtfully, as Ms. Tillman wound her way through the cafeteria, "this could be good."

"What do you mean?" Kathleen asked.

"I mean, maybe what we've needed all along is for someone to tell Ms. Tillman what it's like in McCrackpot's class."

"Come on, Annie," Rosa said, "I think Ms. McCracken is a good teacher."

"Well, you're the only one who does," Annie said. "She drives the rest of us crazy. Just wait until Ms. Tillman hears that McCracken gave her daughter extra work!"

"Are you kidding?" Sam asked. "My mom will just say it's good for me. She probably *asked* McCracken to give me extra work." She shook her head. "Sorry, but I don't think having me in the class is going to change Ms. McCracken."

"It's worth a try," Sharon said brightly.

Sam smiled. "Well, I'll tell my mother the truth. But don't expect any miracles."

Sam was starting to feel pretty good about the girls in her class. At least they didn't hate her just because she was the principal's daughter.

Sam was on her way to Ms. Rivers's class for English when the tall girl with the scar on her lip plunked her hand down on Sam's head and held her in place.

"Slow down, wuss," the girl ordered. "I wanna talk to you."

"What do you want?" Sam asked bravely. She figured that the girl who was holding onto her head was at least a foot taller than she was. And a lot meaner, too.

"I'm Ronnie Smith, and don't you forget it. You think you're so hot, don't you?"

"No," Sam said.

"You think you're gonna get privileges 'cause of your mother."

"Not really," Sam said.

"Yeah, you do," Ronnie insisted. "But let me tell you. I'm gonna even the score. If I see her giving you special treatment, I'm gonna flatten her little, itty-bitty *sweetheart*." Ronnie pulled hard on Sam's hair. "And if you ever tell her anything bad about me, I'm gonna kill you. Got it, flea?"

"Yes," Sam said quickly. "I got it."

"Good." Ronnie shoved Sam hard against a locker and then strode on.

Sam stood for a moment, blinking back tears. No one in her old school had ever hurt or threatened her. The Academy didn't have *thugs*. There was no other word to describe a menace like Ronnie Smith.

Sam went into Ms. Rivers's class too depressed to believe anything would ever get better. She'd just found one more thing to hate about Martin Luther King, Jr., Elementary. Ronnie was a big problem, the kind that didn't go away.

On Friday evening, Sam lay on the living room couch, the phone receiver pressed against her ear.

"So what's that school like?" Danielle asked.

"It's the worst," Sam answered. She'd just spent three whole days in "that school." She'd also spent most of her at-home time trying to convince her mother to send her back to the Academy.

"They don't have computers," Sam explained. "There's no pool or student lounge. They don't teach French until *seventh grade*. The cafeteria serves poison, and everyone thinks I'm weird."

"Do the other kids give you a hard time?" Danielle asked sympathetically.

"There's this one girl, Ronnie Smith, who

threatened to kill me—just because my mom's the principal!"

"How could your mom yank you out of Parkside and put you in some dump where your life is in danger?" Danielle said.

Sam sat straight up. "That's it!" she said. "The one argument I haven't tried yet. At Martin Luther King, Jr., I could be killed! My parents can't ignore that!"

"You really think it will work?" Danielle asked.

"I don't know," Sam said. "But at this point I'm desperate."

Sam found her mother working in her study. Ms. Tillman was frowning at her computer screen.

"Hi, Mom," Sam said.

"Hi, sweetheart," her mother replied in a distracted voice. "I'll be with you in a minute." Her fingers flew over the keyboard, then stopped as she frowned again. "This format isn't working..." she muttered.

"Want me to help?" Sam asked. She was good with computers.

"I'll work it out," her mother said. "Now what can I do for you?"

Sam sat down on the little striped couch across from her mother's desk. "I just thought you should know something, Mom."

"What's that?" her mother asked.

"My life is in danger at MLK, Jr."

"Really," her mother said, glancing at the screen again.

"Is that all you can say?" Sam demanded. "*'Really'*? I'm your only child!"

Ms. Tillman still didn't look alarmed. "We're rated one of the safest schools in the city," she said.

"Maybe the other kids are safe," Sam said. "But I'm not."

"And why is that?"

"Because," Sam said, rolling her eyes, "*my mother is the principal!* That makes me a prime target. People want to kill me."

"Which people?" Her mother was trying to keep a straight face, but Sam could see the amusement in her eyes.

"Lots of kids," Sam said. "But I'm not going to name names."

"Of course not," her mother agreed.

"Well," Sam said, "don't you agree that my life being in danger is a good reason to send me back to the Academy?"

"If I really thought your life were in danger, I *might* agree. But I don't think things are as bad as you're making them out to be." Sam saw that her mother no longer looked amused. In fact, she looked a little angry. "You're not going back to the Academy," she continued. "Don't even waste your time thinking about it."

"I'll talk to Daddy," Sam threatened.

"Go right ahead," Ms. Tillman said. "You can speak to him the next time he calls." She glanced at her watch. "Which should be in about an hour."

Sam did talk to her father that night. She explained. She begged and pleaded. She threatened never to help him with his computer work again. She even gave in part-way, saying she'd stay at MLK, Jr., if he'd just make her mother take her out of McCracken's class.

Mr. Tillman's reply was very clear. "Let it go, Sam. You're staying in that school and in that class. And we won't listen to another word about it."

One week later, Sam gave up. Her parents weren't going to budge. She'd just have to make the best of a terrible situation. If only she didn't miss Danielle and the Academy so much.

Sam hadn't made any friends at her new school. She could still remember the first day of second grade when she and Danielle met.

They'd become best friends instantly. The minute they saw each other, they knew they'd be together for their whole lives.

Why isn't it that easy now? Sam wondered, as she trudged toward MLK, Jr. It was another cold winter morning. The branches of the trees in Harry Park were bare and black against the sky. The hills were covered with a thin coat of frost. Sam's breath came out in little white puffs. She saw other kids cutting through the park on their way to school. They were all walking in twos and threes. She didn't have anyone to walk with. Everyone else already had their friends. It felt as though all the good friends were already taken. Sam had never felt so lonely.

Maybe I bragged too much about the Academy, Sam thought, as the brick school building came into sight. *Maybe everyone in McCracken's class thinks I'm stuck-up. Well, let them. Danielle's still my best friend. Besides, who wants to be friends with MLK, Jr., kids anyway?*

But there was one kid Sam did want for a friend—the boy who sat behind her, Kareem Jackson. Sam had been fascinated by Kareem ever since she realized he was shorter than she was. But it was more than that. As far as she could tell, Kareem was one of the coolest kids in the class. He was really smart. And even though he was small, he was really athletic. Everyone liked him. And Sam wanted him to like her.

The problem was Sam didn't think Kareem noticed her.

He knew she sat in front of him, and that her mother was the principal, but that was it. Sam knew she had to do something to make Kareem want to be her friend.

As soon as Sam decided to do something to impress Kareem, she spotted him leaning against the wall in the schoolyard. He was hanging out with some of the boys in their class: John Jerome, Carlos Santiago, Eric Holland, and Michael Leontes.

"Hi," Sam said, walking up to them.

"Go away," Michael Leontes said. "Can't you see this is guys only? Or are you blind?"

"Lay off, Leontes," Kareem said. "She wasn't bothering you."

"Her face bothers me," Michael said.

"Me, too," said Eric, who was Michael's best friend. "She looks just like the principal."

Sam felt her face getting hot with embarrassment. She wished more than anything that this wouldn't happen to her.

"It's not her fault her mother is the principal," Carlos said. He grinned and held out his hand to Sam. "How's it going?"

"Okay, I guess," Sam said, slapping him five. Part of her felt like a fake. She'd never slapped anyone five in her life. She didn't belong here. She ought to leave. But she also wanted Kareem to be her friend. "What's up?" she asked Carlos, hoping that was the right thing to say.

"We were just talking about McCrackers," John explained. John was Annie Tuzmarti's good friend. Sam decided that he was okay. John liked to tease, but at least he acted human most of the time.

"I was saying I wonder where McCracken lives," Kareem said. "It's kind of hard to imagine that lady living in a normal apartment."

"She probably sleeps in the school office," Carlos cracked.

"Like a vampire," Michael said. "Instead of a casket, she sleeps in a filing cabinet—just waiting for someone to drive a ruler through her heart."

"That's really gross," Carlos said.

"And dumb," Sam added. "McCracken's no vampire. She lives in a house or an apartment like everyone else."

"How do you know?" Eric challenged.

"Her mother probably told her," Michael said.

Sam was about to say, "She did not!" Then she had another idea. "I don't really know where McCracken lives," she admitted. "But I could find out."

"You could?" Kareem asked. He sounded really interested.

"Definitely," Sam said, feeling more confident than she ever had before at MLK, Jr.

"How?" Michael demanded.

Sam didn't have a clue. But that didn't matter. She'd figure it out. "I'm really good at getting into places without anyone noticing," she told the boys. "It's the only good thing about being small."

Kareem grinned at her, and Sam knew she had scored a hit.

"You think you're some sort of spy?" Eric scoffed.

"Sort of," Sam said, but she liked the idea. She'd always snooped on her parents. She was good at listening in on conversations. Once she'd even held some envelopes to a light bulb to read the letters inside. It wasn't very interesting, though. Mostly she discovered that her parents got bills for gas, electricity, water, and a computer magazine.

Michael Leontes stepped forward so that

he was nearly standing on Sam's toes. "Let me get this straight," he said. "You're telling us you can find out where McCracken lives?"

"That's exactly what I'm telling you," Sam said, staring up at him with her toughest expression.

"I dare you to do it by the end of school today."

"Wait a minute—" Carlos said.

But Sam wanted to prove to them all just how cool she was. "Done," she said. "Meet me back here at three o'clock today, and I'll let you in on the secret."

All that morning, Sam thought about how she was going to get McCracken's address. She thought even more about how it was going to change her life. She finally knew how she was going to make herself fit in at her new school. She was going to be the class spy—the one everyone came to when they wanted hot information that no one else could get.

At lunchtime Sam put her plan into action. She ate her sandwich quickly. Then she headed for her mother's office. She knew that today her mother was having lunch with the president of the PTA.

"Excuse me, Ms. Reigert," Sam said to the

school secretary. "Is my mother in?"

"She went out for lunch, Sam," Ms. Reigert answered.

"Would it be okay if I waited for her in her office?" Sam asked. "I have to ask her something."

"Go ahead," Ms. Reigert answered. "She ought to be back soon."

Sam took a deep breath as she entered her mother's office. She didn't dare close the door all the way. She didn't want Ms. Reigert to be suspicious. She waited until she saw the secretary typing.

Please, Mom, Sam thought, *don't walk in now!*

Moving silently, Sam snuck over to the big file cabinet in the corner of the principal's office. Then she opened the drawer labeled FACULTY. And she took out the file with *Miriam McCracken* written across the top in bright orange Magic Marker. Sam held in a squeal of triumph—it had been almost too easy.

At three o'clock that day Sam waited for the boys to meet her in the schoolyard. She was extremely proud of herself. She'd gotten McCracken's address, just as she'd promised them she would.

Kareem and Carlos arrived first. Michael Leontes followed a few minutes later.

"Well, shrimp?" Michael demanded.

"Where are John and Eric?" Sam asked. She wanted all of them to hear the news.

"Eric's got detention with McCrackpot," Michael said. "And John's got karate class. So, midget, did you get McCracken's address or not?"

Sam smiled. "I got it all right. And she doesn't live in a filing cabinet. Ms. Miriam McCracken—"

"Mimi!" Carlos hooted. "I've got your number!"

Kareem laughed. "So where exactly does she live?"

"Somewhere in Parkside," Sam reported. "She lives on Reddington Terrace. Number 63."

"Is that a house or an apartment?" Michael demanded.

"How would I know?" Sam said, irritated. "The file just gives an address."

"You got into McCracken's records?" Kareem asked. He definitely sounded impressed.

"The faculty files are in my mother's office," Sam said proudly.

"What else did her record say?" Carlos wanted to know.

"I didn't have time to read very far," Sam admitted. "My mom was on her way back from lunch. She almost walked in on me. See, I told Ms. Reigert I had to ask my mother a question, and she let me wait in her office."

Kareem gave a low whistle. "Not bad," he said.

Sam gave what she hoped looked like a casual shrug. "I told you, I'm good at this sort of thing."

Kareem's dark eyes seemed to be challenging her. "Well, then I dare you to go to McCracken's house today."

Sam gulped. She hadn't counted on that one.

"Go to McCrackpot's house...and bring back proof you were there," Michael added.

"What do you mean, bring back proof?" Sam asked. "I am *not* breaking into anyone's house."

"You don't have to break in," Michael said, obviously enjoying himself. "Just take something from her porch."

"What if she doesn't have a porch?" Sam asked. "What if she lives in a big apartment building?"

"Then bring back something from the lobby," Michael said. "Use your imagination, termite."

Kareem looked at Sam curiously. "Are you going to do it?" he asked.

Sam wanted to back out, but she couldn't. She knew that if she said no, everyone would think she was a complete wuss.

"Yes," Sam told the boys. "I'll do it."

One hour later, Sam was pacing up and down Reddington Terrace, trying to ignore the biting wind. Getting here hadn't been easy. The street was all the way across town. Sam had taken two buses and then walked for about twenty minutes. Now her fingers were freezing, it was getting dark, and she couldn't find number 63. She'd found numbers 59 and 65. But as far as Sam could tell, numbers 61 and 63 just didn't exist.

This doesn't make sense, Sam told herself. Ms. McCracken isn't the type of person to get her own address wrong. She's too much of a stickler for every little detail. So how could her address be wrong in her file?

Sam decided to take one last walk down the darkening street. Like those on her own street, the houses on Reddington Terrace were mostly brownstones. But this neighborhood wasn't quite so fancy. The houses were a little run-down. There were no gas lamps, and only a few houses had gardens.

For the last time, Sam paced in front of the houses numbered 59 and 65. And then she noticed something she hadn't seen before. Tucked away behind the two brownstones were two smaller brick buildings. They were carriage houses. Once, probably in the 1800s, the owners of the brownstones had kept their horses in those buildings. But later they'd been converted into homes.

Sam approached the first of the two carriage houses. Her heart began to hammer as she read the address on the mailbox: 63 Reddington Terrace. Sam had found McCracken's house!

Sam noted with relief that none of the windows were lit. Ms. McCracken wasn't home yet. She'd lucked out twice in one day.

Now, Sam thought, what can I take back to convince that jerk Michael that I've really been here? Her eyes scanned the front of the house. It was pretty charming, really. A two-story brick house with tall curtained windows and four steps that led to a tiny porch.

Ms. McCracken must like flowers, Sam thought. A group of clay flowerpots sat in one corner of the porch. But it was winter and their earth was bare. Sam thought about taking a pot, but that was serious stealing. She was a spy, not a thief!

What else could I take? Sam wondered.

Then her eyes fell on the mail, half sticking out of the slot in Ms. McCracken's front door. The very top piece of mail was a postcard advertising a new brand of cigarettes.

McCracken would never smoke, Sam thought. She definitely won't need a postcard advertising cigarettes. Sam reached for the postcard and turned it over. Just as she thought, it had McCracken's name and address on it—definite proof. Her mission was a success. Tucking the postcard in her pocket, Sam headed home.

Sam made sure she got to school early the next morning. She couldn't wait to show the boys McCracken's postcard. But no one was waiting outside for her. A cold rain was falling, and the school had opened its doors early, letting the students in before the first bell. Sam hurried inside, where she found Kareem at his locker. He was taking out his books for the morning classes.

"Here," Sam said. She handed him the postcard she'd taken from McCracken's mailbox.

Kareem glanced at it, and his eyes widened. "You really did it!"

Sam nodded. "McCracken lives in a carriage house behind some brownstones on the other side of town."

Kareem smiled at her. "You're all right," he said.

Sam felt proud and happy and excited all at once. She wanted to smile back. She wanted to do cartwheels. Instead she acted super-casual. "It was no big deal," she said, and then started toward her own locker. Very deliberately, she turned back to him. "Just let me know," she said, "if there's anything else I can do."

A few minutes later in McCracken's classroom, Sam saw that her strict teacher was not at her desk. Instead Mrs. Bounder, the school shrink, stood at the front of the classroom.

Mrs. Bounder had a reputation for being a pushover, and everyone in McCracken's class knew it. A group of kids were leaning out an open window, calling down to cars on the street. Michael Leontes was standing on top of his desk, singing a song filled with curse words. And Ronnie Smith and her friends Jodi and Cheryl were playing catch with one of David Jaffe's drumsticks.

Mrs. Bounder clapped her hands for order. "Take your seats, class!" she shouted. "Please take your seats!"

Everyone ignored her until she asked, "Do you want me to tell Ms. McCracken how you're behaving?"

Suddenly, they all took their seats.

Mrs. Bounder looked very relieved. "Now, Ms. McCracken will be a little late this morning. I'm just filling in for half an hour or so."

Michael Leontes started to laugh at this announcement. And though she wasn't sure why, something about the way he was laughing made Sam very uneasy. He sounded almost nasty.

"Please take out your geography books," Mrs. Bounder said. "And begin reading Chapter Eight."

Everyone took out their geography books. They all read about Joshua trees in California's Mojave Desert. Sam couldn't figure out why anyone thought a plant was such a big deal. She was looking at a picture of the funny-looking trees when the classroom door swept open.

Ms. McCracken strode into the classroom, the tip of her nose still pink from the cold. "Thank you, Mrs. Bounder," she said. "I trust everyone has behaved?"

Sam nearly choked as the school psychologist answered, "Oh, they've been lovely."

Mrs. Bounder left the classroom, and Ms. McCracken sat down at her desk. The class watched her. They were all waiting for her to begin the math lesson.

Ms. McCracken took off her glasses and cleaned each lens with a piece of tissue. She put the glasses back on. Then she just sat staring at the top of her desk.

Something is wrong, Sam thought. She didn't know Ms. McCracken very well, but even she could tell that this wasn't normal behavior for their ever-efficient teacher.

David Jaffe put his hand up. "Are we going to do math now?" he asked when Ms. McCracken called on him.

Ms. McCracken took a deep breath. "No," she answered. "I would greatly appreciate it if you would all continue your reading."

Sam's eyes went back to her geography book, but her mind was on her teacher. Something was definitely wrong with Ms. McCracken.

In the cafeteria that day, Sam was surprised to see that McCracken's class had not split off into the usual tables of girls and boys. Instead, everyone was standing around a table at the back of the lunchroom. And they were all talking about why Ms. McCracken had been late that morning.

"Can you believe it?" Carlos said. "It's probably the first time since she was born that McCracken's been late for anything. Oh, Mimi, oh my!"

"'Being on time is a courtesy and a virtue,'" Annie quoted McCracken in a high, nasal voice. Then she stuck her finger down her throat and pretended to gag.

"Maybe she's sick," John Jerome suggested cheerfully. "*Real* sick."

"I've always thought she was sick in the head," Sylvie added.

Rosa looked upset. "Something bad must have happened to her," she said. "I'm worried."

"Why are you worried about that old bag?" Michael wanted to know.

"Because Ms. McCracken's okay sometimes," Desdemona answered. "She's not *always* mean."

"Yeah, well you and nerd-face are the only ones who think so," Michael shot back.

"What could have happened to her?" Jimmy Wong said. "It must have been major."

"I know how we can find out," Kareem said. He looked straight at Sam. "We've got ourselves the perfect spy!"

"Do you think you can find out what happened?" Annie asked eagerly.

"Well—" Sam started. She wasn't sure how she could find out why McCracken had been late.

"Of course, she can," Kareem said. "Sam's got connections. She can find out anything."

7

That evening Sam and her mother sat at the dinner table, eating soup and freshly baked biscuits.

"Mom," Sam said, "do you know why Ms. McCracken was late for class this morning?"

"Yes, I do," her mother answered.

Sam took a spoonful of soup. "Aren't you going to tell me what's going on?"

"No," her mother said, "I'm not. Now, have you done your homework yet?"

"No," Sam admitted. Why was it that whenever her mom wanted to change the subject, she started talking about homework?

"Ms. McCracken tells me you're having a little trouble with math problems," her mother went on. "Do you need help?"

"Oh, great!" Sam said. "You tell me when McCracken says stuff I don't want to hear, but not when she says something interesting!"

"Your schoolwork concerns you," Ms. Tillman explained. "Your teacher's private life does not. If Ms. McCracken wanted her students to know why she was late, I'm sure she would have told you."

"Mom, you can trust me," Sam said, crossing her fingers behind her back. "I'm your daughter!"

"I'm aware of that," her mother replied. "You're also a student in my school. And when it comes to school business, you're a student first and my daughter second."

Sam thought about that for a moment. Then she said, "I don't think I like that. I like being more important to you than anyone else in your school."

Her mother reached over and gave her a hug. "You are and you know it. But I can't treat you differently than I treat other students."

Sam gave a deep sigh. Her mother wasn't going to give in on this. She'd have to discover McCracken's secret another way.

That night, while Sam was doing her homework, the phone rang. Her mother picked it up in the living room. Sam snuck to the top of the stairs and listened carefully. It was Gloria Moreno, the principal of Parkside High and her mother's best friend.

They talked for a while about boring things like school budgets. Then Sam heard her mother say, "Well, Miriam McCracken had a nasty surprise this morning. When she woke up she found her living room window smashed. Someone had thrown a rock through it. The poor woman couldn't come to school until she'd hired someone to repair the window."

Sam remembered Michael Leontes's laughter that morning, and a chill went down her spine. The horrifying truth had just dawned on her.

Michael had thrown the rock through McCracken's window! Sam was sure of it. And it was her fault because she'd given him the address!

All the way to school the next morning, Sam thought about Michael smashing Ms. McCracken's window. How could he have done that? Sam wished she could find a way to tell on him that wouldn't get her in trouble as well.

In the schoolyard, a group of kids from

McCracken's class were hanging out underneath the basketball net.

"Hey, Sam!" John Jerome called out as Sam entered the schoolyard. "Got any more hot info?"

Sam walked toward them slowly. She still wanted to be accepted by them, even if they weren't the sort of people she'd ordinarily be friends with. But she was going to have to be careful from now on. She didn't want to help some jerk like Michael Leontes cause major trouble.

"Did you find out why McCracken was late yesterday?" Kareem asked her.

"Yeah," Sam said in a hushed voice. "Someone threw a rock and smashed her window. She was late because she had to stay home until it was fixed."

"Excellent!" Michael Leontes said.

"Is it?" Sam asked angrily. "Sounds pretty mean to me."

"I mean, that you found out," he said quickly.

"Does McCrackers know who did it?" John asked.

"No," Sam answered. She wasn't going to mention her suspicions about Michael.

"How'd you find out?" Kareem asked.

"I listened in on a phone conversation," Sam answered. "My mom is best friends with the principal of the high school. They tell each other everything."

"You're really great at this spy stuff," Sharon Fuller said in an admiring tone.

"Just like Mata Hari," Desdemona said.

"Mata who?" Sylvie asked.

"Mata Hari was a very famous woman spy," Desdemona explained. "My mother took me to a play about her. Mata Hari was really Dutch, but she said she was a dancer from Java." Desdemona demonstrated an exotic-looking dance step. "Then she spied for both the French and the Germans."

For a moment Sam pictured herself as a glamorous international spy. Sort of like a female James Bond.

"Cool," Carlos said. "What happened?"

"She got executed during World War I," Desdemona said. "It was very tragic."

Kareem smiled at Sam. "Maybe you don't want to be *exactly* like Mata Hari," he said.

"Right," Sam agreed. "I'll do the spying, but I'll definitely skip the part about getting caught."

Ronnie Smith shoved her way through the crowd of kids that had gathered around Sam.

"You think you're so hot, Tillman?" she said. "If you're a real spy, prove it. My grades could use some help. Get the answers to the math test McCracken is giving on Monday."

"Could you?" John Jerome asked.

Sam said nothing. *No!* she felt like screaming at Ronnie. *If you want the answers so badly, steal them yourself.* But when she opened her mouth no words came out.

"She can't," Ronnie said. "She just won't admit it."

Sam wanted to back down. So far, all her spying had been successful. And Sam had been listening in on her parents for years. But stealing answers for a test was a big deal. What would Danielle think if she could see Sam now?

Sam was about to say no way—and then she looked at Kareem, who was standing there gazing at her as if she could work magic. And Sam found that she didn't want to disappoint Kareem. She wanted him to think she was great. It was fun to have a boy for a friend for a change.

"I'll see what I can do," she said in a cool tone.

But inside she was thinking, *Maybe this spy stuff has gone far enough.* Every time she took another dare, she was letting herself in for more and more trouble. If she did what they wanted, she'd be risking everything.

"Ms. Tillman, would you please tell the class the answer to problem number five?" Ms. McCracken said.

Sam stared down at her math workbook. Despite the advanced math she'd had at the Academy, Sam couldn't solve the word problem. And good old Helmet Hair always knew when someone didn't know the answer. It was like radar. As far as Sam could tell, McCracken's favorite sport was calling on kids when they didn't know the answer and totally humiliating them.

"Ms. Tillman," the teacher went on. "Please stand up and read the problem aloud."

Sam stood up and read the problem. It was about a man who had to take three trains because another train was broken. She was supposed to figure out how much longer it took the man to take the three trains instead of the original one.

Sam couldn't believe that anyone cared what the answer was. "I'm sorry, Ms. McCracken, but this is stupid," she said when she finished reading the problem.

"And why is it stupid?" Ms. McCracken asked in an icy voice.

"Because the answer is obvious," Sam replied. "Forget the trains. *Take a cab!*"

Behind her, Sam could hear the other kids laughing.

"Ms. Tillman, I do not find your answer amusing," Ms. McCracken said.

"Well, I don't find this problem amusing," Sam shot back before she could stop herself. "And I don't appreciate your trying to embarrass me in front of the whole class." Sam froze, realizing how awful she'd sounded. It wasn't like her at all!

"Ms. Tillman, you may see me after school today for a detention," Ms. McCracken said. "Now, do you or do you not know the answer to this problem?"

"I don't," Sam said quietly.

"Very well," the teacher said. "You may sit down. Ms. Santiago, do you know how to solve this problem?"

"Yes," Rosa said. She stood up, went to the blackboard, and solved the problem in about three seconds flat. Sam wondered why they didn't just promote Rosa to college and get it over with.

Sam spent the rest of the morning sulking. What in the world was happening to her?

She couldn't believe she'd gotten a detention on a Friday afternoon. She was supposed to meet Danielle after school today. They'd planned to go skating and then get a pizza on Grant Avenue. This was too much. Danielle would think Sam was in prison. Teachers at the Academy never gave Friday afternoon detentions. Actually, they almost never gave detentions at all. Sam would have to call the Academy during lunch hour and leave a message telling Danielle she couldn't make it.

And it was all McCracken's fault! It'd serve her right if I found out the answers to her test, Sam thought. Besides, the whole test would be word problems, which Sam had trouble with. It'd be nice to have the answers to the test. And she was just mad enough at McCrackpot to get them.

The question is *how,* Sam thought, as Ms. McCracken drew a giant Joshua tree on the blackboard. What if McCracken didn't have the answers written down? No, she'd have to. She was too organized to do it any other way.

So the question was really *where.* If the answers were at McCracken's house, Sam would have to forget about the whole thing. There was no way she was breaking in, especially after what Michael Leontes had done. Ms. McCracken had probably bought a guard dog by now. But if the answers to the test were in school, where would they be?

Sam's eyes fell on the file drawer at the side of the teacher's desk. She'd just have to wait patiently until McCracken opened it.

Ten minutes later, Sam had her chance. Ms. McCracken opened the file drawer to take out charts of the plants in the Mojave Desert. Sam immediately raised her hand and asked to go to the girls' room. "It's an emergency!" she said.

"Very well," Ms. McCracken replied.

Sam walked to the front of the classroom and looked inside the file drawer as she passed. The label on the second file read MATH TESTS.

Sam couldn't believe her luck. Mission number four was going as smoothly as the first three. A feeling of power surged through her. Nothing could stop her now.

8

At lunch that day, Sam gathered a group of kids once again.

"Okay," she said. "Who's interested in the answers to the math test?"

"Are you telling us you can get them?" John asked.

"That's right," Sam said. "But I can't do it alone. I'll need two volunteers."

"I'll help," Sylvie said at once. This surprised Sam because Sylvie was kind of a goody-goody.

"Me too," Kareem said.

Sam hadn't felt so happy since she'd started at MLK, Jr. It was almost as if Kareem had just said he was on her side.

"Okay," Sam said. "I need you two to be on lookout. I'll do the hard part."

Sylvie looked very relieved.

"So let's do it," Sam said.

"Now?" Sylvie almost shrieked.

"It's lunchtime," Sam reminded her. "It's the only time McCrackers is out of the classroom. Besides"—she pointed at the cafeteria food on her tray—"this stuff is gross. You don't want to stay and eat it, do you?"

"I suppose the Academy had gourmet food?" Michael Leontes sneered.

Sam didn't want to start bragging about the Academy again. She knew that only made the other kids dislike her. "Never mind that now. Let's get that test. Sylvie, Kareem, are you coming?"

"Definitely," Kareem said.

"I guess," Sylvie said.

Sam, Sylvie, and Kareem left the cafeteria and made their way through the halls.

"My stomach hurts," Sylvie said, as they started up the stairs to the second-floor classroom.

Sam sighed. "Just pretend you're going to your locker to get your coat," she told Sylvie. "It's no big deal."

"Right," Sylvie said. "But what if a teacher stops us?"

"Tell her what I just told you," Sam said.

"But what if she doesn't believe me?"

"Sylvie, you worry too much," Kareem said.

"I know," Sylvie said unhappily. "Everyone tells me that. I can't help it."

"Terrific," Sam muttered. "That's exactly what we need on a mission. A worrier."

"Mission?" Sylvie snapped. "What mission? You make it sound like we're going to stop a war. We're going to steal a math test!"

"Ssshh!" Kareem said. "Do you want the whole school to know about it?"

"Okay, okay," Sam said. "Let's just keep it quiet."

They emerged from the stairwell onto the second floor. Sam looked around. The coast was clear. She motioned for the others to follow. Then silently she made her way toward McCracken's classroom.

"The door's closed," Sylvie whispered.

"I can see that!" Sam whispered back.

"What if it's locked?" Sylvie worried.

Then I can call off this whole thing, Sam thought. She'd be incredibly relieved if they couldn't get into the classroom. She didn't really want to steal a test any more than Sylvie did. *Please, Ms. McCracken,* Sam prayed, *have the door locked.*

Sam approached the door. She reached out and turned the knob. "It's locked," she said, trying to sound disappointed. Inside, she was saying, *Yes! Yes! Yes!*

"Let me try," Kareem said. He tried the handle with the same results.

"Sorry," Sam said. "I wasn't counting on the door being locked."

"It's okay," Sylvie said. She looked as relieved as Sam felt. "We'll explain it to the others."

"Not so fast," said a voice behind them.

Sam's heart sank as Michael Leontes swaggered toward them. "I can't believe you wusses are giving up so easily," he taunted them.

"McCracken locked the door," Sylvie explained.

"So *un*lock it," Michael said, looking directly at Sam. "Aren't you spies supposed to be able to pick locks? You know, use a credit card or a hairpin or something."

"I don't have any credit cards or hairpins," Sam said.

Michael gave her a look that made her feel like a total waste. Then he took a wallet from his back pocket and pulled out a laminated Y membership card. "Try this," he said.

Sam knew she had no choice. She couldn't back down now. Not in front of Kareem.

Trying to look as if she did this sort of

thing every day, Sam crouched down and tried to insert the edge of the card into the keyhole.

"Not like that, you dork!" Michael snapped. "Don't you watch TV? You're supposed to wedge the card between the door and the doorjamb!"

"If you're such a know-it-all, why don't you do it?" Kareem challenged him.

"Because she's the spy!" Michael said. He crossed his arms over his chest and glared at Sam. "Either you get into the classroom, or I'll tell on all three of you."

"Sam!" Sylvie whined.

"All right, all right," Sam muttered. She didn't know who she was more disgusted with—Sylvie, Michael Leontes, or herself.

Sam wedged the plastic card against the lock's bolt. To her amazement, the bolt slid back into the door. And when she turned the knob, this time the door opened.

"You did it!" Kareem said.

"Okay," Sam said, thinking fast, "I'll go get the test. But you two have to keep watch."

Kareem glanced at his watch. "Hurry!" he said. "Lunch period's almost over."

Sam snuck into the empty classroom and made straight for McCracken's file drawer. What if that's locked, too? she wondered hopefully. Then I'll be off the hook.

But the drawer slid open easily. Sam took out the file marked MATH TESTS and began to skim through it. It was a thick file with dozens of tests. And at the very end of it was another file labeled ANSWER SHEETS.

Sam felt her pulse race. Each answer sheet had a separate sheet with the test problems clipped to it. This was excellent! It was exactly what she was looking for! She began to flip through them, sure that she could find the word-problem test. But, to her dismay, she couldn't find it. She began to panic—it just wasn't there! Then Sam turned to the last sheet and there it was. The word-problem test! She nearly dropped the file.

"Hurry!" Sylvie whispered frantically. "Someone's coming!"

Moving quickly, Sam unclipped the word-problem answer sheet from the test. Then she replaced the file and closed the drawer. Handing the answer sheet to Kareem, she locked the classroom door behind her. "Let's go!" she said.

The three of them ran until they were safely back in the stairwell.

"What happened to Michael?" Sam asked.

"He chickened out and ran when he heard footsteps," Kareem said. "He's a coward." He grinned at Sylvie. "How about that? You're braver than Leontes!"

Sylvie smiled shyly at the compliment.

"But I got the test!" Sam reminded him.

Sylvie looked serious again when she examined the answer sheet. "Sam, don't you think McCracken's going to notice that it's gone?"

"Maybe," Sam said.

"Maybe?" Kareem echoed in disbelief. "She's definitely going to be looking for her answer sheet on Monday. Now we've got another problem."

"What problem?" Sam asked, feeling a little irritated. She wanted Kareem to be impressed with her, not *worried*.

"After we've written down the answers to our test," he said, "we've got to get this answer sheet back in McCracken's file drawer!"

Sylvie looked like she was going to cry. "Oh, that's just wonderful. Now we have to go through this all over again!" Just the thought of it was enough to make Sam feel like crying, too.

At three o'clock that afternoon, while all the other kids rushed out of the school building to start their weekends, Sam remained in McCracken's classroom. She sat at her desk while Ms. McCracken looked through some papers on her desk. *What's she going to do to me?* Sam wondered.

At last Ms. McCracken stopped reading. She peered at Sam through her bifocals. "Ms. Tillman," she said. "Do you know why you're here on a Friday afternoon?"

"Because I talked back in class?" Sam guessed.

"That's correct," Ms. McCracken said. "Tell me, did you speak to the teachers at the Academy that way?"

"No," Sam mumbled. *But that's because they weren't such a pain,* she added silently.

"Well, we're not going to start bad habits

here," Ms. McCracken said. She handed Sam several pieces of lined paper. "You may now write 'I will not speak disrespectfully to my teachers.' One hundred times."

Sam gulped and began writing. She couldn't believe this! It was like something from the last century. And this was just for talking back in class. What would happen if McCracken ever found out she'd stolen the answer sheet for Monday's test?

Finally, Sam finished the one hundred sentences. Her fingers were cramped and her eyes felt bleary. Outside, the late afternoon sky was growing dark.

She took her assignment up to the teacher's desk. Ms. McCracken seemed to spend a long time examining Sam's sentences. Sam wondered if she was counting them all.

At last Ms. McCracken looked at Sam. "Your handwriting could be neater," she said.

Sam nodded, not daring to argue.

"I will give you fair warning," Ms. McCracken went on. "If I have to give you a second punishment assignment, your mother will have to sign it. Do you understand me?"

"Yes," Sam said in a soft voice.

"You may go, Ms. Tillman."

Sam left the classroom in record time. The

halls were completely empty. They were so quiet, they seemed a little eerie. Sam grabbed her books and jacket and raced out of the school, eager to get home.

She stopped as she realized that a group of kids from her class were gathered on the playground. Ronnie, Kareem, John, and Rosa were all talking to a young woman with a tan coat and curly blond hair.

"There she is!" Ronnie Smith called out, pointing a finger straight at Sam. "That's the principal's daughter. She's finally out of detention!"

Sam scowled at Ronnie's announcement, but didn't have time to respond. The woman started toward her, smiling.

"Are you Samantha Tillman?" she called out.

"Who wants to know?" Sam asked cautiously. Her parents had taught her never to talk to strangers.

The woman held her hand out to Sam. "My name is Lauren Barnes," she said. "I'm a reporter for the *Parkside Weekly*."

Sam didn't shake the woman's hand. She stood silently, holding her books close to her chest.

"Here," the woman said. She showed Sam a photo ID from the *Weekly*. Then she gave

Sam a business card with her work address and phone number on it.

"What do you want?" Sam asked, still suspicious.

"I'd like to ask you some questions," the reporter answered. "For an article about your school."

"Why don't you ask them?" Sam asked, nodding to her classmates.

"The article is a follow-up to the letter that appeared about a month ago," Lauren explained. "The one that asked why you were attending the Academy."

"I read that letter," Kareem said. "That was the first time I heard about Ms. Tillman having a daughter." Kareem suddenly looked very shy. "I remember wondering what you were like, Sam," he added quietly.

"I read it, too," Rosa said. She smiled at Sam. "It's strange to think we read about you before meeting you."

Sam thought about that. She liked the idea of her classmates reading about her. It kind of made her a star. Maybe it would be okay to talk to this reporter.

"Okay, Ms. Barnes—" she started.

"Lauren," the reporter corrected her. "Please call me Lauren."

"Lauren," Sam said. It felt kind of weird to

call an adult by her first name, but it was fun too.

"Can you tell me why your parents sent you to the Academy in the first place?" Lauren began.

"It's the school that's closest to our house," Sam said. "And when I started kindergarten, MLK, Jr., was pretty rough."

"That was before your mother took over as principal?"

Sam nodded. "My mom was teaching college then."

Lauren jotted something down in a small notebook. "And why did your parents transfer you to public school this year?" she went on.

"For a lot of reasons," Sam answered honestly. "The Academy got super-expensive. And MLK, Jr.'s been a good school ever since my mom took over."

"Did your transfer have anything to do with the letter that appeared in the *Weekly?*" Lauren asked.

Sam felt herself growing wary. What was Lauren getting at? "I think the letter got my parents thinking," Sam answered carefully. "But they were pretty quick to agree with each other that this was the best thing for me."

"But do *you* think it's for the best?" Lauren asked. "How does MLK, Jr., compare to Parkside Academy for Girls?"

Sam hesitated. Part of her was dying to tell Lauren Barnes the truth. She'd just love to tell the world what a total dump MLK, Jr., was. And how McCracken was the meanest teacher in the entire state. But another part of her sensed that that was exactly what the reporter wanted to hear.

"Can *I* ask a question?" Sam asked.

"Sure," Lauren replied.

"Are you trying to do a story that will make my mother and MLK, Jr., look bad? Are you trying to get me to say bad things about this school?"

"No," Lauren said firmly. "I'm looking for the truth. If the truth is that you like MLK, Jr., better than the Academy, that's what I want to hear. Is it?"

"Is what?" Sam asked, confused.

"Is it true that you like MLK, Jr., better than the Academy?"

Sam felt trapped. If she said yes, she was lying. If she said no, she was putting down the school her mom had worked so hard to rebuild.

Sam saw Kareem looking at her, his eyes curious, as if he really wanted to know which school she liked better.

Sam drew a deep breath. "The Academy has some things MLK, Jr., doesn't have," she answered. "Like computers and a swimming pool and a student lounge and good food in the cafeteria. Sometimes I miss that stuff. But I like the kids in my class."

"Very diplomatic," the reporter said dryly. "I have one more question. You know that after the letter appeared in the *Weekly,* the school board had an emergency meeting about you. A lot of people were upset when they realized that Ms. Tillman sent her daughter to private school. How do you feel about having to transfer schools to make things easier for your mother?"

"I—I can't talk anymore," Sam said hurriedly. Lauren's question hit her where it hurt, and there was *no way* she was going to let this woman see her upset. "I've got to go."

"Sam, wait—" Lauren called.

But Sam was already out of earshot, blinking back her tears as she ran toward home, trying to forget Lauren Barnes's last question.

That evening at six thirty Sam put a frozen casserole in the oven and set the table. Her mother had left a message on the machine saying she'd be home at seven. For once, Sam didn't mind her mother being late. It meant she wouldn't have to explain why *she'd* been late. Sam was praying that Ms. McCracken hadn't told her mother about her detention.

At exactly seven, the front door opened and her mother rushed in. "Hello, darling!" she called as she took off her coat. "I'm sorry I'm late again."

"No problem, Mom," Sam called back from the kitchen. "Dinner's ready."

Her mother swept into the kitchen, bent to kiss her, then joined her at the table. "And how was your day today?" she began.

Sam thought for a minute before answering. "Interesting. Definitely interesting."

"I wish I could say the same," her mother said. "I spent all day reviewing school expenses. Really, it's criminal how much food costs these days!"

"Especially when no one can eat what they serve in the cafeteria," Sam added. "It tastes disgusting."

If Sam's mother heard her, Sam couldn't tell. She just kept talking. "Then, just when I realize that I have to request more money for the new computers, the school superintendent calls to announce new budget cuts!"

Sam tuned out as her mother rambled on and on. As if five measly computers were actually going to make a difference. Sam was getting annoyed. She didn't really care about school expenses. Didn't her mother know that? How come a reporter, a total stranger, was more interested in Sam than her own mother was? Sam's mind went back to the interview with Lauren Barnes. Had she been transferred just to make things easier for her mother?

"Sam, did you hear what I just said?"

"Uh—sorry, Mom."

"Honey, you're not paying attention," Ms. Tillman said.

"Well, you're not paying attention to me," Sam retorted. "All you do is talk about your stupid job! You pulled me out of my school and put me in yours, and you haven't even asked me how I like it! You don't care, do you?"

Ms. Tillman looked at her daughter in astonishment.

"Of course I care," she said. "Both your father and I care very deeply about you."

"You just don't have time to show it," Sam said bitterly.

"Samantha, what is all this about?" her mother asked. "What happened at school today?"

"Nothing," Sam said airily. "I just met a

total stranger who's more interested in me than you are!"

"Sam—"

"I want to know something," Sam interrupted. "I want you to tell me the real reason I was transferred to MLK, Jr."

"It seemed the healthiest choice for all of us," her mother replied.

"You mean the healthiest choice for you," Sam shot back. "You just wanted the school board to leave you alone!"

"Sam, I—"

But Sam didn't give her mother a chance to explain. She left the table and walked purposefully up the stairs to her room. She picked up the phone and shut the door firmly behind her. Then she called the one person who would understand the way she felt right now—Danielle.

10

On Sunday morning, as soon as she finished her breakfast, Sam dialed Danielle's number. She didn't care if she woke up the entire Vaughn household. Danielle should have returned her call by now. It was only about the fortieth time Sam had called that weekend. Patiently, she listened to the phone ring five times. Once again, the Vaughns' answering machine picked up to explain that no one could come to the phone.

Sam had already left message after message, telling Danielle to call her. She'd told her it was *intensely* important. Sam needed to talk to Danielle so badly it hurt.

But Danielle hadn't called back. The Vaughns were probably away for the weekend, Sam reasoned. But why hadn't Danielle told her about a trip? What if Danielle was there and just not answering? No, Sam refused to believe that was possible. Her best friend would never let her down like that.

Now Sam left another message asking Danielle to please, please, *please* call her *ASAP!* Then she stomped upstairs to her room and closed the door. She knew her mother wouldn't bother her. She and her mom had barely spoken since their argument on Friday night. Her mother's favorite punishment—The Silent Treatment—was in full force. As usual, her mother was in her study, working at the computer.

Still, Sam moved silently as she crossed the room to her closet and took out the answer sheet she'd "borrowed" from Ms. McCracken. Leaning back against the pillows on her bed, Sam began to read through the answers. She had until tomorrow to memorize them.

Suddenly, Sam sat up straight. "What am I doing?" she asked herself aloud. "What's happening to me?" She'd never stolen or cheated in her life. Now, after less than a month at MLK, Jr., she was breaking into files, stealing tests, and planning to help half the class cheat. "I'm turning into a juvenile delinquent," she said in wonder.

It's my parents' fault, she told herself. If they hadn't made me change schools, I never would have done any of this.

But, deep down, Sam knew she couldn't blame her behavior on her parents. Or even on her new school.

She was losing it. She needed a serious reality check.

She had to talk to Danielle—now!

Sam bundled up and practically flew down the stairs and out of the house. It was a long walk to Danielle's house in the Heights, but she was determined to patch things up with her friend and take control of her life. This cheating thing could ruin her forever at MLK, Jr., if McCracken ever found out. And if she couldn't make it at MLK, Jr., she'd certainly never be accepted back into the Academy when her parents finally came to their senses.

When she saw Danielle, they'd brainstorm some new ideas for Sam's return to the Academy—there had to be a way! A wonderful image came to mind of her and Danielle talking and laughing in the Vaughn kitchen over a plate of oatmeal raisin cookies, freshly baked by Martha, the Vaughns' housekeeper.

Finally, the Vaughns' ivy-covered stone house came into view. Sam couldn't contain her excitement. She ran up to the window and peered inside at the Vaughns' sitting room.

There was Martha, all right. But she wasn't carrying a plate of cookies. She was serving Belgian waffles with ice cream to Danielle—and Mia and Janet and Susie! The four girls were still dressed in their pajamas and were seated on top of their rumpled sleeping bags. There was a roaring fire in the fireplace. The bags were arranged in a circle. The perfect cozy Saturday night sleep-over party, followed by a fancy Sunday brunch!

Sam couldn't believe what she was seeing. It was like a bad dream come true!

Sam was so stunned by the sight of the girls assembled there that she forgot they could see her just as easily as she could see them. Mia saw her first and waved. Danielle looked up, smiled, and came to the door. Sam didn't know what to say or do. There were no words for this bizarre situation. It was the ultimate embarrassment. Way worse than her mother talking to her in public at MLK, Jr. Way worse than McCracken making her look stupid in front of the class.

She'd crashed Danielle's sleep-over party! And Danielle was standing there, inviting her in for waffles and chatting away as if *nothing was wrong with this picture!*

"The four of us are the Current Events News Team for school next week," Danielle

82

explained, "so we decided to get together and figure out our strategy."

But Sam didn't see any evidence of school work being done this morning, or the night before. She'd brought in the Sunday paper herself, from where she'd found it lying outside on the front step. The girls weren't watching CNN, and they looked like they were having too much fun to be talking about anything serious.

There was a makeup kit unpacked on the coffee table, along with a bunch of magazines opened up to the beauty pages. A book of ghost stories lay beside Danielle's sleeping bag. Remnants of popcorn crunched beneath Sam when she sat down, and the girls giggled nonstop as ice cream melted on their faces and ran down their chins.

Janet reached over to wipe Susie's face with her napkin.

"Stop!" Susie squealed. She pushed out her foot to give Janet a swift kick and ended up hitting Sam by accident.

I don't belong here, Sam realized, as she rubbed her sore hip. It's as if I'm invisible. I no longer exist. And that fact made her so sick she refused a serving of Martha's waffles, even though she knew she was insulting the friendly elderly woman by doing so.

"So," Mia purred, "how *are* things going for you over at MLK, Jr.? Why didn't you bring over some of your new friends?"

Sam's mouth opened and closed a few times like a fish before she could speak. "Uh...I'm meeting up with them a little later to...uh...study for a math test. But I just thought I'd stop by and say hi. Since I don't see you all during the week," she finished lamely.

What a joke! Obviously there was no way she was going to get any time alone with Danielle today. And now that she saw her with the other Academy girls, she knew she couldn't talk about what was *really* going on at MLK, Jr. The topic of cheating was as out of place at this party as she was.

Sam realized she had to get out of there—and fast. It wasn't just the fire that was making her sweat.

Excusing herself, she made her way back to Parkside in a daze. Danielle hadn't tried to stop her from leaving. She was probably relieved when Sam took off and ended the awkward visit. The scenery went by in a blur. She was so out of it that a car whizzed by with a loud honk, barely missing her.

As soon as she got home, Sam felt trapped again. Her upset mood turned to anger, and she ran up to her room and slammed the door as hard as she could. She was past caring what her mother might think about that.

I could turn myself in, she thought. *I could give the answers back to Ms. McCracken, and tell the other kids I just couldn't go through with it. Then I'd be in trouble, but at least I wouldn't be a juvenile delinquent.*

But she wouldn't be Sam the Spy either. She wouldn't be the girl Kareem thought was so cool. The very idea of a life without friends made her shudder. She'd never be able to survive it. Sam picked up the answer sheet and uncrumpled it. It was the key to a tough test. It was the key to her popularity.

On Monday morning, half an hour before school began, Sam waited under a big oak tree in Harry Park as Sylvie, Carlos, Annie, John, Michael, Desdemona, Sharon, and Ronnie Smith gathered around her. Sam rubbed her hands together, wondering if the cold weather would ever end. Spring seemed a long way off.

"Okay," Sam began when the whole group was present for their "study session." "We all know the answers to today's math test. All we have to do is choose these eight letters on our tests. Then we all get A's."

Ronnie slapped her hard on the back. "You're some kinda superspy, all right!"

John Jerome didn't look impressed. "Are you sure these are the right answers?" he asked.

Sam held out the answer sheet so John could take a closer look. "Look, these are the answers in McCracken's own handwriting. Do you have a problem with that?"

"I do," Desdemona said in a quiet voice. "I mean, I don't think I can do this."

"Why not?" Sam asked.

"Because if my mother ever finds out I cheated, I'll have to move to another continent," Desdemona answered.

"You gonna snitch?" Michael Leontes demanded.

"*Please*," Desdemona said in a haughty voice. "I have better things to do."

Sylvie looked at Sam in disbelief. "What's going to happen if *your* mother finds out you were in on this?"

"Not much," Sam answered truthfully. "My parents always feel so guilty for not spending more time with me that, when I do something wrong, they usually don't punish me. Mostly I get long, boring lectures or The Silent Treatment."

Sylvie took a step back. "I don't think I

can use these answers," she said. "I'm sorry, but cheating is wrong, Sam. Besides, I'd worry too much about getting caught. I'm getting nervous just thinking about it."

Annie kicked at the base of the tree. "I am, too," she admitted. "I'm not real great at hiding things. McCracken would probably take one look at me and say, 'Guilty!'"

"You are all such a bunch of wusses," Michael declared

"Shut up, Leontes," Kareem said. "Everyone here gets to make their own choice."

"So what are *you* gonna choose?" Michael challenged him.

Kareem shrugged. "I didn't do so well on my last math test. My dad's hassling me about my grades. I need an A. Besides, we went to a lot of trouble to get these answers. I'm using 'em."

"Me, too," Carlos spoke up.

Annie looked directly at John. "How hard can this test be? It's just eight little word problems."

"I'm terrible at word problems," Sam said.

"Ditto," Sharon chimed in.

"I'm terrible at *words*," Ronnie joked.

John thrust his hands into the pockets of his black leather jacket. "Count me in," he said. "I believe in making life as easy as possible."

"You mean you believe in being as lazy as possible," Annie said. John grinned and yanked on a lock of her hair. Annie grinned back and kicked him.

"Careful with the ankle," John said. "It's still swollen from yesterday's ice hockey game."

Sam ignored their bickering. "Kareem's right," she said. "The answers are here. Everyone makes their own choice. No pressure. But there is something I need help with."

"Spelling your name?" Michael jeered.

Desdemona sent an elbow into Michael's ribs. "Oh, I'm so sorry," she said in a high, exaggerated voice. "My elbow must have slipped!"

"Will you guys cut it out!" Sam said. "I have to return the answers to McCracken's file. And I've got to do it this morning. I need someone to set up a distraction and get her out of the classroom for a few minutes."

Desdemona gave a graceful curtsey. "Leave it to me. Drama is my specialty." She frowned. "But I'll need help. This is definitely a two-person distraction."

"John will do it," Annie volunteered.

"I will?" John asked.

"Yes," Annie said. "Desdemona, tell him what to do."

John glared at Annie. "You don't want to live very long, do you?" he growled between clenched teeth.

Sam decided it was time this meeting broke up—before they all wound up fighting one another. "Anyone who wants the answers, copy them now," she said. "Then we'd better get to school. McCracken's going to be suspicious if we're all late."

A mischievous smile lit Desdemona's face. "I've got it!" she said. "The perfect distraction. Sam, John, come here. I'll fill you in on the plan."

But before Sam could listen to Desdemona's plan, Ronnie grabbed her by her jacket collar. "This is just one test. My grades are going to need a lot more help than this. You said you know computers," she snarled.

Sam struggled to get out of Ronnie's grip. "So what?" she gasped. "Let go! You're choking me!"

Ronnie relaxed her grip. "Well, our report cards come out of a computer," she said, her eyes narrowing. "I think your next mission should be to change a few grades."

Sam was speechless. Computer hacking was *definitely* going too far.

Ronnie let go of Sam's collar and shoved Sam so hard she nearly fell over. "You'll figure out a way, Superspy. For now, just think about it."

Kareem gave a low laugh as Ronnie lumbered off. "Superspy," he echoed. "That's some title, all right." His eyes searched Sam's. "You gonna live up to it?"

Sam stared back at him, feeling confused. What did he mean by that nasty remark? He was the one who'd challenged her to get McCracken's address. He'd helped her steal the test, and he was planning to cheat. She knew he admired her for what she'd pulled off so far. So why was he being a big bully like Ronnie?

But Sam didn't have a chance to ask him. Desdemona was tugging on her arm, saying, "C'mon, Sam. First things first. We've got to deal with this math test thing quickly!"

Sam sat at her desk and tried not to fidget. Ms. McCracken stood in front of the class, about to call the roll. Sam's heart raced inside her chest. Any minute now, Desdemona and John would begin their distraction.

They'd better be convincing, Sam thought nervously. They had to get McCracken out of there and give her time to get the answer sheet back into McCracken's file.

Suddenly, the door to the classroom burst open and Desdemona flew in, tears streaming down her face.

"Ms. McCracken," she sobbed. "Please, you've got to come quickly!"

"Pull yourself together, Ms. DuMonde," the teacher said. "Now why are you in such a state?"

"It's John!" Desdemona sobbed. "He's—he's—"

Sam was fascinated. She could hardly believe this was an act.

"What is it, Ms. DuMonde? *Tell me at once!*" the teacher ordered.

Desdemona took deep, heaving breaths.

"It's John Jerome," she said in a wavering voice. "He and me were—"

"He and I," Ms. McCracken corrected her.

Sam rolled her eyes. Only McCrackpot would think about grammar at a time like this.

"He and I were running," Desdemona continued, "'cause we were late. And just as we got to school, John fell. He can't get up now. His ankle is all swollen."

Ms. McCracken frowned. Sam wondered nervously whether the teacher could see through Desdemona's act. But at least John really did have a swollen ankle.

"Please," Desdemona pleaded. "He can't stand up. You've got to come help him!"

"Very well," the teacher said briskly. She gave the class a forbidding look. "I'm going to step out of the classroom for a few minutes. I expect you all to behave perfectly while I'm gone. I suggest you use the extra time to review for your math test."

The second she was sure McCracken was

on her way out of the school, Sam ran up to the file cabinet. She opened the drawer, made sure she had the right file, and replaced the answer sheet she'd taken.

Feeling a little calmer, she returned to her seat. There was always the possibility that someone would rat on her, but Sam had noticed that in McCracken's class, kids usually didn't tell on each other.

A few minutes later, Ms. McCracken and Desdemona returned to the classroom. Desdemona took her seat, looking very relieved.

The teacher fixed the class with a severe glare. "Mr. Jerome is in the nurse's office having his ankle bandaged," she announced. "We'll wait for him to arrive and then begin the math test."

Ten minutes later, John limped into the classroom, and Ms. McCracken handed out the math tests. Sam felt perfectly relaxed as she zipped through the answers. The hardest part was looking as if she were actually trying to figure out the problems. Sam was almost humming, she was so pleased with herself. With a little help from her new friends, she'd pulled it off. She *was* a superspy!

Sam finished the test and didn't even bother to check it over. She was home free!

The next morning when she got to school, Sam saw Annie and Sharon huddling together on the edge of the playground.

"How'd it go yesterday?" Sam asked, walking up to Sharon.

"It was the easiest math test I ever took!" Sharon replied.

"That's because you had all the answers," Annie pointed out, her teeth chattering. "You didn't really take it."

"Who cares?" Sharon said. "All that matters is I finally aced a math test. Sam, I owe you one."

"Hey," said Kareem, coming up to them. "What's up?"

"We were just talking about the math test," Sam said. She waited for Kareem to tell her how great she was. She wanted him to thank her and tell her he'd be grateful to her for the rest of his life. Instead, Kareem snorted loudly. Sam couldn't help thinking he sounded like a pig.

"That was a real waste," he said.

"What do you mean, *a waste?*" Sam asked indignantly.

"I mean, we went through all that trouble,

and they weren't even the right answers," he said in a disgusted tone of voice.

"They weren't?" Sharon asked, amazed.

"You didn't notice?" Kareem asked her. "*You* must have noticed," he said to Sam.

Sam's eyes widened in horror. She'd just circled the answers she'd memorized. She hadn't even bothered to read the questions.

"You mean you *used* those bogus answers?" Kareem asked.

Sam nodded. Maybe, just maybe, Kareem was playing a joke on her.

"You'd better hope the others were smarter than you two rocket scientists," Kareem said. "Because if McCracken gets a bunch of tests with identical wrong answers, she's gonna know there's something funny going on."

"Wh-what did you do?" Sam asked.

"I worked out the problems," Kareem said. "I probably won't get an A. But I won't flunk either."

The bell rang then. It wasn't a joke— Kareem was telling the sad, sorry truth. Sam headed into school with her feet dragging. She couldn't believe this disaster was happening right in the middle of her life.

"I will now return yesterday's math tests," Ms. McCracken announced to the class.

Sam felt sick.

"Rosa Santiago," Ms. McCracken called. Rosa went up to the teacher's desk, took her test paper, and smiled.

Does she *ever* get anything besides A's? Sam wondered.

She carefully watched the faces of all the kids as they walked back with their tests. Kareem, who'd said he hadn't used the answers, looked pretty neutral. John, Carlos, and Michael looked bored. Ronnie wore her usual scowl. Sam couldn't really tell what grades any of them had gotten.

But Sharon was different. The minute she took her paper she burst into tears.

"Please take your seat, Ms. Fuller," Ms. McCracken said unsympathetically. She held out the next test. "Ms. Tillman, your paper."

Maybe I should leave right now, Sam thought. Maybe I could go live in Danielle's closet. Slowly, she stood up and went to get her paper from McCracken. Now she understood why Sharon had burst into tears.

At the top of Sam's math test was a big red F. And next to the F was a bright red stamp that read: *I have examined my child's test paper.* Beneath that sentence was a line that said *Parent's Signature.*

For the first time in her life, Sam had failed a test. And her mother had to sign it!

But Ms. McCracken wasn't finished making Sam's life miserable. She cleared her throat. "Ms. Fuller, Ms. Tillman, and Mr. Leontes, please see me after school today."

Sam sat in McCracken's classroom and watched the minutes tick by on the clock. It was five minutes after three. Ms. McCracken was out in the hallway, talking to another teacher. Sharon was sitting a few seats away from Sam, looking as though she were about to be executed. Michael sat at the front of the room. He kept turning toward Sam and running his finger across his throat. Sam tried to ignore both of them.

But she couldn't stop thinking about taking the test paper home for her mother to sign. What would she say? What would her father do?

The door to the classroom opened, and Ms. McCracken came back inside, her heels clicking against the wooden floor. She leaned against her desk and fixed her students with one of her extra-sour looks.

"I understand that any one of you might neglect your studies and fail the math test," Ms. McCracken began. "What I can't understand is how the three of you managed to fail with identical answers. Which is quite amazing, considering what those answers are. Ms. Tillman, please read us your answer to the first problem."

Kareem called this one right, Sam thought, as she took out the test with the big red F across the front. She took a deep breath, but it didn't help. "A supermarket cashier rings up a tab for sixty-four dollars," she began, trying to keep her voice from shaking. "The customer leaves the store. The next day the customer returns a can of coffee that cost four fifty-nine, and a roll of paper towels that cost ninety-four cents. She substitutes a roll of paper towels that costs eighty-seven cents. How much money should the customer get back?"

"And your answer is?" the teacher asked.

Sam felt herself blush as she read the answer aloud.

"C: seven billion dollars."

It was totally ridiculous.

"You'd make a very generous cashier," Ms. McCracken said. "I imagine the store you worked for would go out of business in very short order."

Sam wanted to die right now, at the young age of eleven.

"Mr. Leontes, you will read problem two with your answer. And Ms. Fuller, number three, please."

Sam listened as Michael and Sharon read equally ridiculous answers to their problems.

"I think," Ms. McCracken said when they were done, "that we can agree on a few things. None of you is unintelligent. Yet you all picked the most absurd choices possible for your answers. Which means that either you all wanted to fail or you all cheated, using the wrong answers."

Sharon immediately burst into a fresh round of tears. Michael sat there with his usual bored expression on his face. Sam wondered what was going to happen next. Part of her still couldn't believe she'd been caught. Sam tried to calm herself. After all, her mother was the principal. What could a teacher possibly do to her?

"Ms. Tillman," the teacher said, "would you like to explain why the three of you have identical wrong answers?"

"No," Sam answered in a very quiet voice.

"Surely you don't think it's a coincidence?" Ms. McCracken asked.

Sam stared down at her desk and said nothing. She knew McCracken was trying to get her to confess or rat on someone else. And she wouldn't do either one.

She listened numbly as the teacher questioned Sharon and Michael. They didn't crack either.

Finally, Ms. McCracken said, "Very well, you may each write a one-page essay, explaining why you cheated. Your parents will sign it along with the tests. In addition, for the next month you'll each get extra math homework problems."

"But I already get extra homework!" Sam protested.

"Obviously you don't get enough," Ms. McCracken told her. "Busy minds don't have time to cheat. Get started on your essays now, all of you."

Sam stared at the blank page for a long time before beginning her essay. There was no point in lying any longer. It was all over. She was glad writing was easier for her than word problems. She didn't have much energy left for this task.

Finally, she wrote:

I cheated on this math test because I have trouble with word problems. They're hard to solve. And they always sound kind of dumb. I think the people in the word problems shouldn't get in those situations in the first place. But also I was lazy. I didn't want to study. The main reason I cheated was because I wanted the other kids to think I was cool. They think I'm a goody-goody because of my mother. I had to prove they were wrong. This probably wasn't the best way to prove myself. I feel like an idiot now and will not cheat on a test again.

Sincerely,
Samantha Tillman.

When Sam finished her essay, Ms. McCracken stamped it with her red stamp that said: "PUNISHMENT ASSIGNMENT. Parents Sign Here_____." Then she gave Sam twenty extra math problems— ten because she was supposed to be doing more advanced work in math, and ten for cheating.

Outside, Sam found Sharon and Michael waiting for her. She'd never admit it to her classmates, but writing the essay had felt good. She'd gotten all those bad feelings off her chest.

Sharon was in tears again. "My parents will *kiiiiilll* me!" she wailed.

Sam felt awful. She wasn't so worried about herself, but she didn't want Sharon to get punished. "I'm sorry," she said. "I never meant for anyone to get in trouble."

"Then why'd you give us the answers to the wrong test?" Michael demanded.

"I thought it was the right one," Sam explained.

"Well, it wasn't," Sharon sniffed.

"I know that now," Sam said. When were they going to let up? "I guess everyone except us figured that out. Even Ronnie Smith."

"No way," Michael said. "I bet Ronnie was just too dumb to memorize the wrong answers the way we did."

"What are we going to do now?" Sharon asked.

Michael shrugged. "No biggie. I'll get my older brother to sign our papers."

"You think that will work?" Sharon asked,

frowning. She looked doubtful.

"Not for me," Sam said. "McCracken knows my mother's signature. I'd never get away with faking it."

"Well, I will," Michael said. He gave Sharon an annoyed glance. "And you will, too. Stop crying, okay?"

Sharon nodded and wiped her eyes.

"Thanks for all your help, loser," Michael said to Sam. "Remind me never to listen to you again. C'mon," he said to Sharon, "let's go find my brother."

Sharon gave Sam a guilty look. But she didn't even say good-bye.

Sam was left standing by herself. She *did* feel like a loser. Her great plan to become popular was a bust. Even nice kids like Sharon weren't speaking to her anymore. And, honestly, Sam couldn't blame her.

Sam felt lonelier than she could ever remember feeling. Becoming more depressed by the second, she started home. Now she had to tell her mother she had cheated on a test. She wondered briefly if she could forge her mother's signature.

No, Sam decided. I'm in enough trouble. Now is the time to come clean—even if it means a year of The Silent Treatment.

13

That evening Sam waited nervously for her mother to come home. As usual, her mother was at another one of her endless meetings. Sam made herself dinner and did all of her homework—including her twenty extra math problems. She even straightened up the kitchen and living room. And all the while she became more and more nervous. How was she ever going to explain the mess she was in to her mother?

It was almost ten o'clock when Ms. Tillman finally came home. She looked frayed and exhausted. Sam waited until her mother had fixed herself a bowl of soup. Then she said, "Mom, I've got to talk to you."

"Not now, honey," her mother answered. She was sitting at the kitchen table. The bowl of soup was on her left. On her right was a list of figures.

"It's kind of important," Sam pressed on.

"Samantha, I'm tired, I have a headache, I can barely see straight. And I have to start next year's budget. Can't this wait?"

"Not really," Sam said. She gathered up all her courage, then shoved the essay and the test onto the table in front of her mother. "Could you just sign these?"

"Fine," her mother said. Barely glancing at the papers, she scrawled her name across them and gave them back to Sam. Sam couldn't believe it! She'd gotten away with it! Her mother didn't even know what she'd just signed!

It took all of Sam's self-control to walk quietly away from the table—and not race up the stairs, shouting with joy. "'Night, Mom," she called.

"'Night, sweetie," her mother called back.

Sam had just reached the top of the stairs when her mother's voice rang through the house. "Wait a minute, young lady! Let me see those papers I just signed!"

Sam froze and scrunched her eyes shut.

"Come back down here!" her mother ordered. "At once!"

Moving as slowly as she could, Sam walked back down to the base of the stairs, where her mother stood. Ms. Tillman held out her hand. Sam gulped and gave her the essay and test paper.

It seemed to take forever for Sam's mother to read through them. Sam couldn't bear to watch. She stared at the wooden floorboards. She wished she could disappear through a trapdoor and shut it safely behind her.

At last, her mother took a deep breath and said, "Come into the study, Samantha. You and I need to talk."

Miserable, Sam followed her mother into the study. She sat down on the striped couch and finally looked her mother in the eye. All she could tell was that her mother looked tired—and kind of sad.

"Well?" Ms. Tillman demanded.

Sam didn't know where to start. "I-I guess it's like I wrote in the essay," she said. "I cheated on the test."

"If you think getting in trouble at MLK, Jr., will get you sent back to the Academy, you're wrong," her mother said angrily.

"I didn't think you'd send me back to the Academy," Sam mumbled. "I don't really want to go back there, anyway."

"Then why did you do it?"

Sam gave an uncomfortable shrug. "I wanted the other kids to like me. They all thought I was going to be a goody-goody. I cheated on that test because of you."

"Don't you dare blame this on my job!" her mother snapped. "Cheating is wrong. It's not fair to the other kids in your class who've worked hard for their grades. It's not fair to your teacher. And most of all, it's not fair to you. If you don't do the work, you don't learn. And if you cheat on a test, the teacher can't tell whether or not you need help with the material. No excuse makes cheating right. Do you understand me?"

"Yes," Sam said. She quickly added, "I'm sorry."

"Are you?" her mother asked.

"Totally," Sam assured her.

"I wish I believed that," her mother said. "But I honestly don't know if I can trust you anymore. Cheating is a form of lying. It seems my daughter is a liar."

Sam winced. She knew she deserved that, but it hurt.

"Go to sleep, Sam," her mother said in a tired voice. "I can't deal with much more of this right now. We'll talk about your punishment in the morning."

"Punishment?" Sam echoed. "You and Dad never punish me!"

"Well, obviously it's time we started," her mother said. "We'll discuss it in the morning."

All that night Sam tossed and turned in her bed. She wondered what her mother was going to do to her. It took her so long to fall asleep that when she finally did, she slept straight through her alarm.

The next thing Sam knew, her mother was sitting by her bed, shaking her awake. "Get up, Sam," she said. "I've got to leave, and you've got to be out of the house in thirty minutes."

Sam sat up and rubbed the sleep out of her eyes.

"Are you still mad at me?" she asked.

"Furious," her mother replied. "I'm going to have to take very severe action."

"Like what?" Sam asked, trying to sound brave.

"For starters, you've lost your allowance for the next month. You can also consider yourself completely grounded for the next two weeks. That means I want you to come back here directly after school every day. No TV, no videos, and no going out on the weekends either. Each day you'll get a list of chores to do. Today's list is on the refrigerator. You've also lost your phone privileges for the next three weeks. No calls in and no calls out."

"Mom, that's prison!" Sam complained.

"How can you do this? It's just not fair!"

"Neither is cheating," her mother replied. "Think about it!"

Sam got angrier and angrier as she walked to school that morning. She didn't blame her mother for grounding her. Or even for taking away her allowance. But no phone calls for three weeks? That was going too far.

The sound of a car horn brought Sam out of her thoughts. A smile lit her face as she realized it was Danielle's limo honking.

The limo glided to a stop by the curb. The back door opened. "Want a ride to school?" Danielle asked.

"Definitely!" Sam answered, and climbed in. Danielle sat on the back seat, wearing her Academy uniform.

"Hey, brat!" Henry called.

"Hi, Henry!" Sam called back happily. It felt so good to be back in the limo with Danielle again. It felt as though she were stepping back into her old life. Maybe there was still hope for their friendship. Danielle probably wanted to apologize for that awful scene at her house.

"So what's up with you?" Danielle asked.

"Everything!" Sam answered. "I got into trouble at school. Now my mom's grounded me and taken away my allowance and phone privileges."

"Oh," Danielle said. She was quiet for a minute. Then she asked, "What did you do?"

"I cheated on a test and got caught," Sam said, softly. "Actually, that's why I came over to your house that day, to talk about it."

Danielle wrinkled her nose. "Well, I'm glad you didn't bring it up in front of everybody. Cheating is gross," she said. "It's like...sludge."

"Sludge?" Sam echoed.

"You know, like, slimy and disgusting and it sticks to you forever," Danielle explained. "Cheaters are, like, really low life forms."

"Gee, thanks," Sam said. "That's really helpful."

"Well, I just don't think you should cheat," Danielle said, sounding a little huffy. "Is that what everyone does at MLK, Jr.?"

"No, it's not what *everyone* does at MLK, Jr.," Sam replied tensely.

Danielle yawned. "Look, it's not your fault you have to go to a sludge school."

Sam wanted to tell Danielle that MLK, Jr., wasn't a sludge school. Except, deep down, part of her still thought it was. Danielle took a brush out of her bag and began to do her hair. "Guess what? My mom's got a job on St. Thomas during spring break. Mia may come with us." Danielle gave Sam a sideways glance. "I'd have asked you, but your school vacation is a week later than ours."

"Oh," Sam said. She felt like telling Henry to stop the car so she could get out. She'd heard enough. But just then the limo pulled up in front of Martin Luther King, Jr. "Here you are, brat," Henry announced.

"Later," Danielle said, as Sam started out of the car.

"Yeah," Sam said, though she had a pretty good idea she'd never ride in the limo again. She got out of the car and watched it glide off toward the Academy. What was with Danielle? Sam wondered. When did she become such a major snob? Had Danielle changed? Or had *she* changed?

Sam felt someone bump her shoulder. "Nice transport," Michael snickered. Before Sam could come up with a sarcastic retort, she saw Lauren Barnes walking toward her.

"'Morning, Sam!" Lauren called out in a cheery voice.

"Hi," Sam said. She wasn't really in the mood to talk to the reporter. She was still mad at her mom, and she was kind of mad at Danielle, too. She was feeling very crabby.

"Now this is interesting," the reporter said. "The principal of a public school sends her daughter to school in a limousine."

Sam was about to explain that her mother had nothing to do with the limo. But something inside stopped her. After all, she was still furious with her mother for being so mean.

"Do you ride to school in a limo every day?" Lauren asked.

"Yes," Sam lied. The lie made her bold. "My mother doesn't think the neighborhood is safe," she went on. "She always sends me to school in a limo."

Lauren raised one blond eyebrow. "I thought you told me that one of the reasons you were going to MLK, Jr., was that the Academy was getting too expensive. How is it that your parents can't afford the Academy but *can* afford a limo?"

Sam gave the one answer that she knew would really get her mother in major trouble. "I'm not sure," she told the reporter. "But I think my mom said something about taking the money from school funds."

Before Lauren Barnes could ask another question, Sam raced inside the school.

14

"Are ya gonna do it?" Ronnie Smith growled.

It was lunchtime. Ronnie had Sam pinned against the brick wall in the playground. She wanted to know if Sam would get into the school computer and change her grades.

Sam knew that she wasn't going to do it. Still, saying no to Ronnie just didn't seem like a good idea at the moment.

"I don't know if I can," Sam told her.

Ronnie pushed Sam's head up against the brick. "I can do that a lot harder," she threatened.

"I'm sure you can," Sam said. As Ronnie got ready to smash her, Sam began to talk fast. "It's not that I don't *want* to help you. It's just that it wouldn't be easy. You'd have to be an expert hacker."

"I thought you were a spy!" Ronnie breathed in her face. Ronnie had really stinky fish breath and spat her words.

Behind her, she heard Kareem laugh. "Aw, Ronnie, let her go. She's being straight with you. Getting into the school computers is like getting into Fort Knox. You have a better chance of getting A's by studying."

Ronnie let go of Sam. For a moment, she stood with her hands on her hips and glared at Kareem. But she didn't punch him. She just turned to Sam and said, "Later, flea," before she lumbered off.

Kareem's eyes met Sam's. "You like getting into trouble, don't you?" he said with a grin.

"I guess so," Sam said with a sigh. "It's been hard changing schools."

Kareem nodded. "But being a spy is cool."

"It was," Sam said. "Till it got me in so much trouble. McCracken's giving me *twenty* extra math problems a night. And my mother's cut off my allowance and my phone and TV privileges. Plus she's grounded me."

Kareem gave a low whistle. "You're not really going to break into the school computer, are you?"

Sam grinned. "I could use my mother's home computer. I do that all the time. I know she's linked up to the school. But I wouldn't try to change grades. Even if I could figure out how, it'd be a really bad thing to do."

"Kind of like spying," Kareem agreed.

"What do you mean?" Sam asked indignantly. "I thought you liked me being a spy. You're the one who dared me to get McCracken's address."

Kareem raised his hands in the air. "I know, I know," he said. "I've been thinking about all of that. I've been meaning to apologize."

"For what?"

"For pushing that stupid spy stuff," Kareem answered. "I helped you get into the mess of trouble you're in now."

Sam looked at him, not understanding. "I don't get it—"

"It's like this," Kareem said. "That day when you first told us you could get info— what I liked was how you stood up to me and Leontes and Ronnie. You were thinking really fast and could scheme as well as any of us. You're smart and tough for an Academy girl and that's cool. I didn't expect Ms. Tillman's daughter to be any of those things."

"What did you think I'd be like?" Sam asked.

Kareem laughed. "I guess I pictured you in pink fluffy dresses, with your hair tied up in pigtails."

"Right." Sam made a gagging motion.

"Exactly," Kareem agreed. "Anyway, you turned out to be okay. You even pulled off things no one else could. But then I started thinking about what a spy does, and I thought, I don't want to be friends with someone like that."

Sam looked at Kareem in exasperation. "You just lost me again. What are you talking about?"

"I'm talking about how a spy is someone who betrays people. A spy is someone no one trusts, 'cause she'll always sell them out to someone else. You can't be friends with a spy, because one day she'll stab you in the back."

"I'd never stab you in the back," Sam said.

Kareem gave her a sheepish smile. "No," he said, "you don't seem like the type. That's why even though you're smart and all, I'm not so sure you want to be a...superspy."

They both laughed.

"Omigosh," Sam said suddenly.

"What's wrong?" Kareem asked.

"I got angry and tried to stab someone in the back this morning. I think I'd better try to undo it fast before anything horrible happens."

"Who'd you try to stab?" Kareem asked.

Sam gave him a weak smile. "My mother," she replied.

Sam glanced at her watch and waited for someone to answer on the other end of the phone. Lunch period would be over in about two minutes, and she was standing at a pay phone on Grant Avenue. She was trying to reach Lauren Barnes. She had to stop her from printing that phony story about the limousine money coming from school funds!

Finally the ringing stopped. "Hi," said a recorded voice. "This is Lauren. I can't take your call right now, but leave me a message and I promise to get back to you!"

"Lauren, this is Samantha Tillman," Sam began. "It's *intensely* important that I talk to you today. Could you meet me after school? It's about my mom and the limo." Sam hung up the phone and breathed a sigh of relief.

She'd talk to Lauren today and stop the story before it was even written. If she was lucky, it would all work out.

Then Sam felt a claw-like hand fasten on her shoulder. And a familiar cranky voice asked, "Ms. Tillman, would you like to explain what you're doing off school property in the middle of the day?"

"I—uh—I had to make a phone call," Sam stammered.

"Why didn't you use the pay phone by the office?" Ms. McCracken asked.

"I forgot it was there," Sam said. "I mean, I haven't been in this school very long."

"You've been here long enough to know that you're not supposed to leave school property during lunch," Ms. McCracken replied. "I certainly hope you weren't planning to meet anyone after school today. You'll be in detention with me."

Sam sat in the auditorium that afternoon, waiting for an assembly to begin. She decided she was doomed. Here she was, trying to do the right thing, and she got in trouble. She had to go to McCracken's detention later today. Which meant she'd miss Lauren Barnes. The reporter would never know she had lied. She'd print the limo story, and her mother would get fired from her job. Her mother would never, *ever* forgive her for this one! Briefly, she wondered why they were having an assembly today. All she knew was that after the first hour of reading, Ms. Rivers had taken their class to the auditorium. As far as Sam could tell, the entire school was there.

To Sam's surprise, it was her mother who walked onto the stage; it still felt weird to see her up there. More than anything else, she didn't want her mother to get hurt.

"Good afternoon, everyone," Ms. Tillman began. "I called this assembly because I wanted to talk to you about our Community Service Program.

"As some of you may know, the program started as an alternative to punishment," she explained. "When students are sent to my office, I often allow them to volunteer for community service. Some of our students have helped with Meals-on-Wheels. Others have worked with disabled children at the library crafts program. Still others have helped clean up Harry Park. I want you to meet some of the people you've helped."

Sam watched, intrigued, as people took the stage to talk about how the students from MLK, Jr., had improved the quality of their lives. An elderly woman said that the kids who delivered her meals were becoming her good friends. A park officer talked about what a difference the cleanup project made in Harry Park. A man from the Salvation Army talked about how the students had helped sort used clothing for people who can't afford new clothes.

Finally, Ms. Tillman took the stage again. "I'm pleased to announce that we're going to expand the Community Service Program," she said. "We're going to add more projects. And you can volunteer for one of these new projects without getting sent to my office. For example, we'll work with the animal shelter to take pets to visit people in nursing homes."

That sounded pretty cool to Sam. She'd definitely like to do that—if she didn't end up grounded for the rest of her life.

"Another group will make toys for kids in the hospital. Others will collect food donations for the homeless. All of these groups need volunteers. I'm hoping you'll all help."

Sam watched in amazement as her mother managed to get at least half the audience excited about the program. Lots of kids were raising their hands and asking questions. Others were ready to sign up right away.

My mom is doing really good things, Sam realized. And I'm about to destroy her if I don't get to Lauren Barnes fast!

15

It was four P.M. before Sam finally got out of the school building. She'd just written "I will not leave school property during the day" two hundred times. She came to an abrupt halt when she saw Lauren Barnes sitting on one of the front steps.

"You waited!" Sam said in surprise.

"Well, you said it was urgent," the reporter said. "Your friend Kareem told me you had a detention." Lauren gave Sam an understanding smile. "You've been getting a lot of those lately, haven't you?"

Sam sat down beside Lauren. "I got this one for going to a phone booth on Grant to call you," she said.

"Sorry. What's so urgent?"

Sam swallowed hard. "I lied to you this morning. My parents don't send me to school in a limo. Ever."

"I know," Lauren said quietly.

"You do?" Sam asked.

Lauren winked at Sam. "A good reporter always confirms her facts. So I checked out the license plates of the limo. Turns out it's registered to the fashion model Kendra Vaughn. You used to go to school with her daughter, right?"

Sam nodded. "Danielle is—I mean was—my best friend."

"Now I've got a question for you," Lauren said. "Why'd you lie about your mom?"

"I was mad at her," Sam said.

Lauren gave a soft laugh. "I once called my grandmother and told her my mother was out all weekend with her new boyfriend and hadn't left any food in the house!"

"Was it true?" Sam asked.

"Well, my mom was dating a man I didn't like. She'd only gone out for a couple of hours, and there was plenty of food in the house."

"So what happened?" Sam asked.

Lauren chuckled. "My grandmother was no fool. She said she knew my mother better than that, and if I lied like that again she'd tell on me." The reporter looked at Sam thoughtfully. "Are you still mad at your mom?"

"Mostly I'm mad at myself," Sam admitted. "I've done some really dumb things lately."

"It must be hard to go to a school where your mother's the principal," Lauren said.

"Actually, I'm finding out she's a really good principal. She's got all these projects going where kids help out in the community." Sam looked at Lauren hopefully. "Maybe you could write an article about that."

"I'll check it out," Lauren promised. "Want a ride home?" she asked. "I haven't got a limo, but—"

"That'd be great," Sam said, and followed the reporter to her car.

Minutes later, Lauren pulled up in front of the Tillmans' brownstone. Sam felt a wave of dread sweep through her. The lights were on. Her mother was home.

"Thanks for calling, Sam," Lauren said. "I appreciate your wanting to tell the truth."

"You're welcome," Sam said, "but I'd better go now."

"Are you in trouble?" Lauren asked.

Sam nodded. "I was supposed to come straight home after school."

Lauren smiled and shut off the car's motor. "Tell you what," she said. "As one ex-liar to another, why don't you let me help you out on this one? I'll tell your mom you're late because I held you up with an interview. It *is* the truth, after all."

Sam smiled. "Thanks, but I think I'd better handle this one myself. I've got to take responsibility for what I've done. I think that's the point my mom's trying to make with those community projects. You can print that, by the way!"

Sam showed up early for school the next morning. After the talk she'd had last night with her mother, she felt better about everything. It was a relief not to be hiding things anymore. And it was the first time since breaking into her mother's file cabinet that Sam didn't feel like a major creep.

"Hey, Superspy!" Ronnie called out as she came up to Sam. Sam's stomach did a somersault.

"I'm out of the spy business," Sam told her.

"How come?" Ronnie asked.

"I didn't like it," Sam answered.

"Are you some kind of midget goody-goody now?" Ronnie demanded.

"Maybe," Sam answered. Suddenly it didn't matter to her whether anyone thought she was a goody-goody. All that mattered was that she felt okay about herself again.

"Hey, Sam," Kareem said, deliberately

stepping between her and Ronnie. "What's up?"

"Ronnie was just telling me I'm a midget," Sam said.

Kareem grinned. "We midgets have to stick together."

Sam grinned back. She knew now she could survive without friends. But it was much better to have at least one good one.

Kareem bounced the basketball he held in one hand. "Want to shoot some hoops?" he asked Sam.

"Sure," Sam said.

It felt great to leave Ronnie standing there in the dust as she walked toward the hoop with Kareem. He loped ahead of her toward the net, dropped his books on the ground, and sank a hook shot. Then he whirled around and passed the ball to Sam on a bounce.

Sam caught the ball and gazed up at the hoop high above her head. "You know," she said as she took her shot, "things are definitely starting to look up."

Don't miss the next book
in the McCracken's Class series:

McCracken's Class #8:
SASHA'S SECRET BOYFRIEND

"I guess I had this idea that you wanted to be Johnny's girlfriend or something," Annie told Sasha. "Isn't that crazy? Sorry I went ballistic before. I think this flu still has me in a crabby mood. I'm sorry, okay?"

"No problem," Sasha said. "Thanks for calling."

"Sure. See ya in school tomorrow."

Sasha hung up the phone and looked down at the little glass ball on the kitchen counter. The fake snow had settled at the feet of the deer inside the ball. It was so beautiful. And so thoughtful of John to give it to her. Now she knew for sure that John wasn't just cute and funny. He was sweet and sensitive, too. And best of all, he liked her. Maybe even more than he liked Annie.

Sasha bit her lip. She couldn't accept John's gift. Annie's friendship meant more to her than her crush on a boy.

Didn't it?

Riding Academy

If you love the kids in McCracken's Class, you'll want to meet the girls at the Riding Academy, too! Join Andie, Jina, Mary Beth, and Lauren as they find fun, friends, and horses at a boarding school with an extra-special riding program.

Riding Academy,
a new series from Bullseye Books,
coming Spring 1994!